Lab

By Sian Rosé

Copyright © 2021 Sian Rosé

All rights reserved.

The characters and events portrayed in this book are fictitious. Any similarity to real persons, living or dead, is coincidental and not intended by the author.

No part of this book may be reproduced, or stored in a retrieval system, or transmitted in any form or by any means, electronic, mechanical, photocopying, recording, or otherwise, without express written permission of the publisher.

A note from the author

Hello readers, and many thanks for choosing this story for your literary consumption. This book is the third and final in a series and is the sequel to my earlier 2020 novels 'Farm' and 'Circus.' For the best experience, I would suggest reading the first two books before this one if you haven't already. You can read for FREE on Kindle Unlimited here: https://www.amazon.co.uk/dp/B08CF21HZ7

Just a quick disclaimer! This book is **NOT** for the faint of heart or for those who are easily disturbed. In fact, it's more extreme, graphic, and brutal than its predecessors (and that's saying something.)

Take note, dear reader, the story is entirely fictional and does not in any way reflect my own personal or religious beliefs. Everything in this book has been wholly fabricated for your entertainment.

If you are offended easily, my advice would be to put the book down and dispose of it accordingly.

If you are still with me, I hope you enjoy the ride, and please know what you thought by leaving a review!

I am so grateful and delighted that you chose to read my work!

Thank you!

Sian R

Faith

It's almost midnight. Svelte, inky darkness surrounds the car; its vast blackness studded with tiny, romantic diamonds. The full moon shines in through the windscreen and bathes our poised lips in a ghostly glow, and I become all the more aware of how close he is to me.

I can breathe him; smell him; touch him, and taste him.

My heart drums rapidly inside my chest, beating almost uncontrollably as I struggle to contain my urges.

"Come inside…" I finally whisper breathlessly as the soft skin of his mouth grazes mine. "Now," I add firmly.

He doesn't need telling twice.

Despite the unspoken three date rule, no sooner have the words escaped my lips, he has unclipped his seat belt and removed his keys from the ignition of the car in one swift motion.

Alive with anticipation, I follow his lead and slip out of the car, carelessly slamming the passenger-side door behind me. Giggling like a pair of lovesick teenagers, we stagger and stumble up the long gravel driveway that stretches out in front of my house. He grabs my arse with greedy hands, and the tip of his tongue whips at the skin on the side of my neck. His warm, minty breath sends a jolt of electricity shooting down my spine, and my skin breaks out in fresh goose flesh.

"You are so fucking hot…" he breathes in my ear.

I smile. Sometimes that's all you need.

Someone to grab your arse and tell you you're hot.

Inside, the house is basked in darkness. We don't bother to switch on any of the lights, our silhouettes dancing silkily in the gloom. I let my clutch bag fall to the floor and promptly collapse like a lifeless puppet into his arms, just as the front door slams shut behind us.

In his big, strong arms, he carries me, my feet dragging along the ground as he devours my face, and I feel the long, rigid probe of his cock digging into my upper thigh. I shiver with pure pleasure.

He drives me into the wall, ripping aside my underwear, gripping tightly onto my bare thighs as he grunts and groans with anticipation.

I hear the jangle of his belt as he goes to release the buckle. However, the sound of the catch releasing is interrupted by a loud, intrusive creak of a stair behind him.

Before I can even blink, his definitive shadow becomes a messy blur as he is ripped away from me, and his figure goes crashing down to the floor. I flail through the air and land flat on my backside, my mouth falling open with shock as I attempt to readjust my vision.

"FUCK!" he screams. Gone is the manly demeanour. His voice is high-pitched, broken, and sharp like a dying child in agony. It's like razor blades being shoved into my eardrums.

Hastily, I scramble to my feet.

"No!" I shriek, finally mustering myself into action. "STOP!"

His shouts and cries of pain and terror quickly become muffled by the horrendous echoes of ripping and tearing that resound through the air. A splatter of something warm and thick erupts into the atmosphere and spatters one side of my face.

"Oh no…" I mutter, shaking my head. My heart sinks as I realise it's too late.

I turn on my heel and slope off back towards the light switch while hungry gobbles and pants continue to drown out his pain and stain the now stagnant air. With a defeated sigh, I flick the familiar light switch by the front door and blink as an orange glow suddenly fills the room.

Silence.

Groaning, I rub the back of my neck and force myself to turn back to look at the damage.

It's bad.

Not worse than usual, but still pretty fucking terrible.

A pair of eyes are fixed on me. A large, lumpy body full of unusually shaped flesh shudders, suddenly still.

I take a step forward and blink again and again as the bright splatters of red sting my retinas.

"Why?" I moan, shaking my head in disbelief. "Why, Beau? Why do you do this?"

I stare at him then. Hopeless.

His eyelids still flutter, but his eyes are already dead. They are still. His broad shoulder has been ripped open as easily as the soft pastry of a jam doughnut, and out of it spills shattered shards of bone and cartilage. Quickly, my eyes flit over the rest of his body, assessing the damage, seeing if there is anything left that could be of any use…

There's a lot of blood- but most likely from mainly superficial wounds… I chew my lip curiously and take another step forward. I see then that one of the main arteries in the side of his neck has been ruptured and severed.

That'll be the cause of death, then.

Straddling his corpse is my daughter. Her head bows. She doesn't speak, but I can tell she is ashamed. All at once, she is no longer a young woman- a beautiful, bright sixteen-year-old. Now, she is just a tiny three-year-old again, looking guilty after being caught with the new pet kitten half dangling from her mouth, its bloody white tail jutting over her lips.

The idea had been that hopefully, the cat could teach the child something about compassion, although clearly, it was a wasted sentiment.

There are more creaks on the staircase, and soon we are joined by Hope.

She narrows her eyes and glares through the bannisters down at the mess that her sister has made. I hold my breath.

"Don't think for one second that I'm cleaning that up," she snaps huffily, folding her arms as she sinks down onto one of the steps. Defiantly, she juts out her chin and turns her face away as if in demonstration.

Sighing, I rub my forehead.

Who knew what a total and utter stress teenage girls would be?

"Beau, why'd you do this?" I ask my older daughter again, more gently this time. Surprisingly, aggression never works with her. She is still hunched over the fresh corpse; scarlet spit reins swooping from her lips, smudges of blood smeared across her chubby cheeks.

Predictably, her eyes fill with tears, and soon a big, fat droplet is rolling down one side of her lumpy, deformed face. My heart instantly melts, all traces of frustration vanishing immediately.

"Oh, come here, darling," I kneel down beside her, uncaring that the pool of blood on the floor is saturating my new satin dress. I coil an arm around her and coax her towards me. "Don't cry," I soothe.

Hope makes retching noises on the stairs, then peers through the bannisters down at me. I send her a sharp warning glance over Beau's shoulder.

"M-m-m-mummy…" Beau mumbles into my shoulder, her warm saliva dribbling over my skin as if she were still just an infant.

I don't mind.

"It's okay, sweetheart," I whisper gently into her ear.

Hope lets out a high-pitched bark of laughter before descending the staircase two at a time, her pretty face pinched into a sarcastic scowl. She stops at the foot of the stairs, just a metre or so away from Beau and me, glaring down at us as if she is the mother and we are the naughty kids.

"Okay?" she repeats, almost spitting the word out in a vicious snarl. "Okay? She just murdered a bloke in our hallway!"

Beau begins to whimper. I hold her oversized, quivering torso close to me.

"She was hungry," I explain to Hope patiently, keeping my voice calm. I've learned that getting angry doesn't work. Not with either of my girls.

"Uh…" Hope tosses a long, blonde plait over one of her shoulders, "so get an apple or order a pizza! Not kill some random guy, then expect everyone else to clean it up!"

Her words sizzle on my skin. I know it isn't fair. And it's not like Beau can help clean up herself. She is always eager to try, however with her big hands and lack of fine motor skills, more often than not, she just makes the mess even worse.

"H-h-h-hope," Beau begins to sob. Roughly, she pulls away from me and clambers up onto her feet towards her sister.

Hope, who is only fifteen, stands at about 5ft 2. Her sister Beau, however, is about triple the size of her and towers above her like a giant. She always has done. Like a monster, she looms over her, big arms outstretched, blood-stained drool still leaking from the corners of her mouth.

"Hope… sorry…" Beau offers pitifully, jiggling her hands about in the air in front of Hope.

Hope tuts loudly and rolls her eyes again.

"No, Beau. I'm pissed off with you. How many times have I told you no more killing in the house? If you're going to rip people to shreds, do it someplace away from here…."

There's no concealing the disgust in her tone. I feel poor Beau shudder, and I feel the shame that radiates off of her.

"It's safer for her to do it in the house," I can't help but come to her defence. Hope shoots me daggers with her eyes, but it's true. At least when this happens at home, it can be swept under the carpet.

"For god's sake…" mumbles Hope, rubbing her temples. She pauses. I can tell that she is succumbing. Like me, she can never stay mad at Beau.

Reluctantly, my slender, blonde-haired teenager steps forward and wraps her spindly arms around Beau's waist. Beau gladly hugs her back, lifting her tiny frame up off of the floor.

A warm glow burns in the pit of my stomach, and I feel my face dissolve into a wide smile.

Suddenly, I've forgotten all about the man. I can barely even recall his name. I'd wanted sex. As I've gotten older, my libido has become insatiable- however, no man could ever fulfil me as much as this… just simply being here, in my lavish home, with my family.

My girls.

My beautiful, perfect daughters.

I step forward to join their embrace and take my time breathing in their familiar scents. It soothes me. Comforts me.

Reality cruelly snatches away our moment of sentiment when I start to feel blood oozing around my bare foot. I groan as I remember the mutilated dead man lying sprawled in our hallway and reluctantly pull away from Beau and Hope. I try to meet Hope's eye, but she avoids my gaze.

"Go on, Beau," she says under her breath, through gritted teeth. "Go upstairs. Put on some Peppa Pig. I'll be up in a bit," she gestures towards the staircase and firmly pats her sister's forearm.

Obediently, Beau gives a little squeal of joy at the mention of her favourite cartoon heroine and proceeds to ascend the staircase.

Hope and I watch as the funny girl clambers up each step, making just about as much noise as humanely possible. We wait until she has disappeared from the top landing of the stairs until we speak.

"This can't keep happening," Hope whispers to me. She pushes past and stands over the leaking corpse, putting her hands on her hips as she grimly surveys the carnage. "Just look at this."

I do.

There is no mess quite like that of a dead, ravaged body, especially when the kill is unplanned and has taken place in an inconvenient spot.

"I've been wanting to get a new carpet anyway," I say finally, even though I only remodelled the house just six months ago. "We'll move him into the back of the van- I'll take him to work tomorrow. If we get started now, we can pull up the carpet and scrub the floorboards...."

"Stop," Hope interrupts me, holding her head in her hands. "Mum, I can't live like this anymore. Why can't you just admit that we need help? This isn't normal...."

The truth burns like a corrosive substance on my lips, niggling away at the tender flesh there.

But I keep my mouth shut.

Hope knows enough. For now.

She knows that her mother is a world-famous animal-rights activist and the founder of a multi-billion-pound cruelty-free chain of laboratories.

She knows that my cosmetics, my sanitary products, and even my medicines are general household names all across the globe.

She knows that she has an older sister who is... mentally challenged and who is prone to random bouts of violence.

She knows that sometimes I use the... *remains*... of Beau's little accidents to aid my research and my practice.

Guilt pinches the inside of my rib cage as I watch Hope disappear into the kitchen, then return a short time later with two pairs of kitchen gloves and a plastic container filled with industrial cleaning products.

What would she do if she knew the truth?

What would she do if she knew that Beau wasn't just born crazed and murderous?

What would she do if she knew that it was me who made her that way?

Hope

"Hope! Hope!"

I nod half-heartedly at my sister and give her a thumbs-up as she clumsily lifts up a soggy piece of paper that is saturated with sickly brown paint. It looks like shit. Beau's 'artwork' often does.

A tired sigh escapes me as I shift about on the cushioned window seat in Beau's bedroom and let my bare foot graze the polished floorboards.

She's sitting hunched over at a bright orange plastic table which is far too small for her. Underneath her weight, the stubby chair legs wane slightly, threatening to snap at any moment. If this wasn't my reality, perhaps it'd be comical. A huge oaf of a human crammed onto a tiny chair at an equally tiny table, finger painting.

Obviously, Mum did try to get Beau to choose an adult-sized art table. But Beau was insistent. She wanted the bright orange one in the shop. And whatever Beau wants, Beau gets.

And if she didn't?

I couldn't tell you what would happen- the eventuality has never arisen. However, judging by her ever-growing body count, I don't suppose the consequences would be pretty.

Briefly, I turn and press my forehead against the cool glass. I look over the long, luscious stretch of emerald lawn and squint as the glorious sunshine stings my eyes. A jolt of apprehension turns my stomach when the harsh, shrill dong of the doorbell resounds through the house, causing the window pane to vibrate against my skin.

"Bell!" cries Beau in alarm.

Rolling my eyes, I sigh and get to my feet. Her deformed, lumpy face is frowning in confusion, the dripping paint brush still hovering mid-air in her child-like grip.

"It's okay, Beau," I tell her patiently, "it's Mummy's friends. Remember? The friends who are going to come and stay with us."

She blinks at me uncertainly.

After hours of scrubbing blood from the walls and hauling the dead weight of Mum's boyfriend's corpse into the van, I finally managed to convince her to get help. Someone to come and share the burden of taking care of my sister. Someone who could hopefully put a stop to her random murderous sprees.

"It's fine. Come on," I cock my head and stick my hand out. "They're very nice people."

Frankly, I haven't a fucking clue whether or not they are nice people. Not really. But I suppose they'll be whatever my mum pays them to be.

Reluctantly, Beau drops the paintbrush and mirrors my movements, slowly getting to her feet. She slopes over and takes my hand, almost crushing the bones in my knuckles with her tight grip.

As I lead her from the room, I chat to her about how Mummy's friends are so excited to meet her and will do lots of painting, cooking, and other fun stuff with her. At the mention of baking, Beau throws her head back and lets out a high-pitched squeal of delight.

"Calm down silly," I rub my thumb on the top of her hand. I can't have her getting all giddy with excitement and freaking the carers out at this crucial, early stage. "Remember to be really polite and show them your pretty smile," I add.

At that, she shows me a toothy, decidedly, *un*-pretty smile.

I love my sister. Of course, I do.

But to say she is a liability is an understatement.

She's a scorned two-year-old locked inside the body of an oversized man. On drugs. Who experiences constant, insatiable urges to kill. It's not exactly a winning combination.

As we approach the top landing of the final set of stairs, I hear the sound of the front door clicking open and a low huff of a breeze blowing in from the outside.

"Oh my god!"

My mum's voice lifts a decibel or two.

Beau and I descend the steps, her podgy, sweating hand still gripping on tightly to my fingers.

Mum is standing in front of the open front door, half inside the house and half leaning out of it. Her arms are wrapped around someone, and I see an unfamiliar pair of hands on her back, fingers entwining in her jet black curls, returning the embrace.

For a split second, I pause. I hadn't realised that these people that were coming were people my mum actually knew. I'd only said that to try to stop Beau from flipping her shit. But judging by the squeals of recognition echoing up the stairwell and lingering in my eardrums, the people at the door were old pals of hers. Certainly, *not* just hired help.

"Come on, Beau," I say under my breath, tugging at my sister's wrist. I lead her down the steps to see my mother letting a huge man about three times my size passing her in the door frame. His face is worn and creased, tanned and beaten by the weather, but still attractive in a rough and rugged way. I notice that, even though Mum is already greeting the person behind him, his wide, deep eyes remain fixed tightly on her.

Behind the giant is an impossibly skinny woman with a face that looks deflated. Her eyes are ringed almost black, framed with deep crows' feet that she's poorly caked in makeup. She also hugs my mother and plants a kiss on her cheek, flashing me a curious look over her shoulder with her bright blue eyes.

Then, hovering awkwardly a few paces back, stands a boy, maybe only a little older than me. He's hot. Obviously so. Like a blonde, floppy-haired heart throb you might see in a boy band. His dark grey eyes meet mine, and I curse myself as I feel my cheeks burn red with embarrassment.

"Hi." The tall guy is now standing directly in front of Beau and me. I sense my sister quiver and rub her hand with my thumb. Normally, I'd be worried.

Beau is unpredictable, to say the least. I'll never forget the time Mum paid for us to have backstage passes at one of Beau's favourite singers' (Harry Styles) gigs. When she met the guy, she'd immediately lunged forward and began beating the living shit out of him for no apparent reason. Mum had to pay a fortune just for them not to press any charges.

However, the man in front of us is so big that he's actually taller than Beau. Although it'd be a tough fight, I'm pretty certain that he could take her down if he needed to. I begin to relax.

"Hi," I smile, squeezing Beau's hand encouragingly. "I'm Hope. This is my sister, Beau. You must be...." I trail off because my mum hasn't said jack shit about who these people are. There was me assuming I was going to meet a handful of carers in miserable, grey uniforms and ugly but practical shoes. But these people are dressed in normal clothes. No… not even normal clothes, expensive-looking clothes. The same brand, I can't help but notice that my mum buys. The renowned designers that won't make anything that so much as lays a finger on an animal in any stage of the production process.

The man doesn't take offense, or if he does, he doesn't show it. He clears his throat and eyes Beau up and down. A smile stretches out on his face, but something about it seems forced as if he is a puppet and someone is pulling at the corners of his mouth.

"I'm Arlo," he introduces himself in a low, husky voice. He clears his throat, "me and your mother go way back."

So, clearly, this Arlo is in love with Mum.

It's so obvious. He may as well have started dry humping her the moment the front door opened.

"This is Dawn," Arlo continues, gesturing to the skinny woman who now stands beside him, her pupils hungrily flitting between Beau and me as if we are some fascinating exhibit at a zoo. She gives me the creeps.

"No," growls Beau, furrowing her eyebrows at Dawn.

I laugh weakly and stroke her forearm. "She's got a great sense of humour," I lie through my teeth, hoping that my mother at least had the sense to pre-warn these friends of hers.

Dawn doesn't bat an eyelid and reveals a stained yellow, sickly-sweet grin in response.

"You don't remember me, Beau?" she asks, apparently undeterred. "I used to take care of you a lot when you were a little baby," she says. "Along with D. You and he were born around the same time," she nods backward towards the teenager who is now crossing the threshold into our home.

I stifle a giggle.

"It's true, Beau-Beau," Mum has turned around now and is standing beside Dawn. "When Mummy had to go and do some important work, Dawn used to take care of you."

She must sense the doubtful frown that involuntarily crosses my face. "Back when I lived on the farm."

Since before I can even remember, Mum has recounted us with stories of this farm. A supposedly magical place where she took care of animals without actually slaughtering them for their meat.

My mum is crazy about animal rights.

That's how she got so much money by making products that are entirely cruelty-free and out-selling all of her competitors ten times over.

There is an entire community of millions and millions of vegans and activists that would literally pay thousands just to sit in a muddy field and listen to my mum speak for half an hour.

It's mind-blowing.

But, also irritating.

If she, or any of her fans, found out that I occasionally sneak the odd cheese burger from McDonald's, I think she'd personally grind me up into human mincemeat

"Ah, right." I nod in polite recognition. In between Dawn and Arlo, the boy in the doorway stands, still staring at me. Behind him stands a figure I didn't notice before. A dark-skinned man with a black beard and eyes that look dull and empty, like murky waters void of life.

"Girls, this is D, and this is Phoenix."

D's pupils continue to bore into me, whereas Phoenix won't make eye contact and continues to stare aimlessly at a space on the carpet. I realise that he's older, maybe about the same age as my mum. So why is he loitering around in the background like an awkward teenager?

"Pleasure," I say.

"It's all mine," winks D, playfully poking out a tongue, flashing a metal ring between his teeth.

Well, *he* seems like a dick.

"Why don't we all go into the conservatory," Mum suggests. "Have a smoke? I've got the most amazing dairy-free cheese…."

My friends think it's fucking awesome when they come over, and my mum just casually offers around spliff as if she's pouring out cups of tea. For me, it's like the novelty has worn off. Besides, there's nothing worse than being stoned and Beau having one of her meltdowns. Controlling her behaviour is exhausting enough, let alone when your limbs feel like solid concrete, and you're just getting into an old-school episode of *Spongebob*.

Pig

I'd braced myself.

I'd been bracing myself for the entire journey, for seeing Faith and her daughters. It's been so long, and yet I could never forget every minuscule inch and detail of that crazy bitch's face.

Sure enough, when I first saw her again, it was as though no time had passed at all. She looked exactly the same as she did back then as if she was somehow miraculously immune to aging like the rest of us. Just the sight of her teasing, mischievous grin sent a shockwave of horror rippling down my spine.

As for the daughters... it was like looking at a pair of ghosts.

Both of them are so reminiscent of their father.

Especially the younger one. She's effortlessly beautiful, and I'm sure, just as charming, funny, and clever as her arrogant shit-head of a dad. I wonder if she also inherited the selfishness, the evil, and the sadistic tendencies of her deranged mother.

I suppose I'll find out later.

The bigger one- the one we are supposed to be assisting with- is still monstrous in every sense of the word. She's huge and mutant-like, as though she is a cartoon as opposed to a real-life human. Her face is horrifically deformed, her skin blotchy and stretched over a multitude of hideous lumps and bumps to an uncomfortable bursting point.

But still, I can see Kevin in her.

He's there, somewhere beneath the surface, his malevolent soul living on through these vessels like a disease.

Needless to say, no amount of mental or emotional preparation could have adequately equipped me for seeing them. It doesn't matter that I've been living comfortably, albeit against my will, for the last thirteen years. Some wounds never heal, no matter how much time passes. They remain open and sore, just as fresh as the day they were first inflicted.

"Phoenix… that's an interesting name." Hope, the younger, blonde one, says to me, rousing me from my daze. I realise that she has held back behind the rest of the group, having passed her older sister's hand over to her mother. The young teenager looks up at me. Beyond the polite interest reflected in her irises, I see a subtle sort of desperation. A desperate urge to win our approval. No doubt because she so badly wants us to stay and somehow eradicate the issue of her sister.

She must really have no idea who her mother is and the hold she has over us.

Faith leads Arlo, Dawn, and Daddy up the corridor, chatting away as though she never went away. Hope blinks at me, her long eyelashes fluttering as she appears to soak me in. For a moment, I wonder how involved she is with Faith's… business endeavours. She's so young, so seemingly innocent. But surely, not even a woman as sly and twisted as Faith could hide her dirty secrets from her own children.

Awkwardly, I clear my throat and force my feet to move so that I am following on behind the group. "Thanks."

I don't mention that it's not my real name; rather, it's a stupid, half-arsed replacement for me to use, just while we're here. Normally, they fondly refer to me as Pig. It feels like an eternity ago that anyone actually called me by my real name, Abdul.

"So, were you a volunteer on the farm too?" Hope asks.

I notice, as we travel further down the corridor, the sickly aroma of incense, so strong that it stings my nostrils and makes my eyes water.

"Yes," I lie. Millions of gruesome, blood-soaked images streak through my mind then. The hours spent scrubbing glistening puddles of human waste from stone floors; hacking through rough, rigid flesh; slicing through limp, lifeless limbs, and being sprayed with hot, stinking blood.

It's true. I worked at the farm.

But no part of it was voluntary.

I could tell Hope the truth, but it seems unlikely she'd take my side. Besides, if I uttered even the tiniest, subtlest word of warning and any of the others caught on, I'd be, to put it simply, totally fucked. I'd either be brutally tortured and made to die a horrific, slow-burning death or alternatively stripped of my privileges as the longest surviving prisoner and kicked out of the house that was my cage. The idea of being tossed back to live on the farm, stuffed into small, suffocating cages drenched in shit, blood, and piss, is more sickening, more terrifying to me than even the thought of dying. There is no fucking way I'm going back to that.

"You aren't a big talker then?" smirks Hope. Her eyes twinkle, and she reminds me of her father in an instant. My old boss who was so smug and so effortlessly charming that he was able to turn everything into some light-hearted folly. *That's* what got me into this mess in the first place. An overwhelming wave of irritation comes over me then, and I feel my fingers twitch with the desire to smack the teenager around the face.

Thankfully, we finally come to an open archway leading out into a vast, open-plan conservatory room. The glass ceiling is sloped downwards, exposing the brilliant blue sky stretched out above. Huge, plush sofas face inwards to a low, antique coffee table that contains a glass bong and an assortment of ash trays.

"Make yourself at home," Faith gestures to the seats kindly. Even *I* get a warm smile from her. I wonder, for a crazy moment, if maybe she's changed. Or maybe I'm just insane. Maybe I imagined all of that awful, hair-raising shit that happened such a long time ago. It's more likely that she's forgotten me altogether and maybe assumes I'm just a new recruit roped in for the ride.

We all sit down. It's then that I notice the huge, hand-painted canvas that hangs on the only painted wall, taking up the majority of the surface. In its centre, a long, pointed face stares morosely down at us- cold, grey eyes gazing, dark hair flopping over a pale, slanted forehead.

"What a gorgeous picture," says Dawn, nodding sadly at the hanging wall art.

Faith sighs and smiles sadly. "My baby brother is always with me," she says, placing a hand on her chest.

Sundance. Faith's younger brother killed himself because he couldn't cope with his sister's deranged life choices anymore. I catch Hope sharing her mother's sad look and wonder how much truth she really knows about her mother's past.

The next hour or so passes quickly. Everyone smokes weed apart from Beau, who lays on the laminate flooring and watches cartoons on a tablet. Drugs never used to be my thing, but now I take as much as I can get whenever the opportunity arises. Who fucking wouldn't, in my shoes?

Truthfully, there isn't a single moment that I wouldn't rather be unconscious.

I don't speak much. Hope seems to have given up trying to coax a conversation out of me and has diverted her attention towards Daddy. Or 'D' as they are referring to him. They speak in low voices, their bodies creeping further together on the couch opposite the other three.

Faith, Arlo, and Dawn chat amongst themselves like old friends. As if Faith didn't suddenly disappear off of the face of the earth sixteen years ago. Arlo talks to her about the farm and the circus. He lies through his teeth about how both businesses are thriving and how the family has never been stronger. Since Faith signed everything over to him, there's no way she would know otherwise. However, an amused flicker in her pupils tells me that she sees through his bullshit. There's a lot that can be said about Faith; she's sneaky, calculating, and downright unhinged. But alas, no one can dispute her intelligence, which is why I sense a tension emerge in the room whenever somebody lies to her.

That's the other thing about Faith.

You don't get away with crossing her.

No-one does.

In an effort to change the subject, Dawn gushes over the house and Faith's pharmaceutical business and the following that Faith has accumulated. She's totally licking her arse, and it's bordering on desperate. I wonder if Faith realises that Dawn's back on hard drugs.

It seems fairly obvious to me. Dawn looks like total and utter shit. Apparently, though, Faith doesn't give a jot about the failing businesses or the fact that Dawn is one line or injection away from a deviated septum or collapsed artery. After a few joints down, she steers the conversation in the direction of the oversized baby sprawled out on the conservatory floor at her feet.

"So if you guys take the job," she begins- I stifle a laugh because there is no *if* about it- "you'll be taking turns to look after Beau."

"What kind of care does she need?" Dawn wonders out loud.

Faith shrugs, "just general day-to-day stuff… she's no trouble, really…."

At that, Hope coughs loudly and raises her eyebrows at her mother. "Mum," she says sternly.

More tension sharply bends the atmosphere. It feels obscene to hear anybody reprimand Faith in any shape or form, let alone this short, skinny child. Even Daddy, who has never even met Faith, has heard enough stories to look increasingly nervous.

"Well, yes, she has a few issues…" admits Faith with a sigh, not so much as batting an eyelid.

Hope purses her lips nervously, and her eyes flit from me to Arlo, to Dawn. She's hopeful. Anxious.

"She can be… violent…" she tells us hesitantly.

"She's killed," adds Faith casually.

"Mum!" gasps Hope, her mouth falling open in horror. It's almost amusing to see how horrified her mother's blunt admission makes her. It quickly becomes evident that Hope hasn't a fucking clue about what Faith is capable of or the ties that connect her to the rest of the family. Otherwise, why would her pretty eyes be almost popping out of their sockets, full of fear that one of us will spring up and call the police?

"It's okay, we can trust them," Faith assures her daughter, "otherwise they wouldn't be here…."

As if on cue, Beau suddenly flings her tablet across the room and begins stomping her feet on the ground. Her face flushes red and contorts into an ugly knot. "Hungry!" she grumbles.

Whilst Arlo and Dawn look on in badly concealed repulsion, Hope sighs and rises to her feet, leaving her half-smoked joint in one of the crevices of an ash tray. "Come on then, Beau, what will it be for lunch?"

D gets up too. "Here, I'll come with you. I'd love to get to know Beau a little better."

I expect Hope to flash him a look of admiration at this heroic gesture; however, her face remains still and expressionless. Indifferently, she shrugs. "Fine. Let's go, Beau."

The young girl's history is scrawled plainly all over her face.

I've gotten very good at reading people over the years, after having spent so much time just sitting in corners… watching… listening.

Hope has been shielded from the dark monster that lurks beneath her mother's polished surface. To her, they're just a normal, rich mother and daughter who could be living a perfect existence if it wasn't for her mentally and physically abnormal older sister. She's grown tired of caring for Beau and likely covering up for her. She resents her mother, even without knowing the full extent of her brutal and bloody crimes.

Beau clambers clumsily to her feet and is led out of the room by her sister whilst D trails smugly behind. Some guys might be put off by Hope's dismissive attitude, but D sees it as a challenge. He is cocky and arrogant. And it's no wonder. He's just sixteen and has already shagged about half of the female population in the family.

Once they're out of earshot, Dawn leans in curiously. "So… Hope knows about your work?"

Faith shakes her head and bites down on her lip. "Not all of it."

"But she knows about the farm?" Arlo whispers, "she knows about the mission? And the family?"

"Not in so many words," admits Faith. She lights up the end of another spliff. "About five or so years ago, Beau started to behave very aggressively. She's just as passionate as me, but unfortunately, she is unable to control her impulses. I thought maybe she was just copying me… maybe it was an affliction towards meat-eaters, but I've come to realise that she doesn't discriminate…" she pauses to take another toke. "Honestly, the number of times she's almost gotten herself locked away…." Faith shakes her head, dismayed, before bringing the joint up to her lips again.

"So you basically need us to babysit?" Arlo asks. "To make sure she stays out of trouble?"

Faith laughs humourlessly, "it's more than babysitting. My daughter is a force to be reckoned with…" she pauses to take a long drag, then slowly exhales the milky white clouds. "But just imagine how great she could be. All that power… all that passion…" she passes the joint to Arlo. "She has so much potential. But with everything else going on, I can't train her up by myself." When she says it, she looks like she is gulping down sandpaper, as if the words are physically painful for her to say.

She isn't a woman who is accustomed to admitting defeat.

Dawn nibbles on her scabby lower lip. "So… what do you want us to do, Faith?"

"I just need support," Faith replies. "I need back-up…" she reaches over and places a dainty hand on top of Arlo's. "I need my family," she smiles.

I resist the urge to retch.

"Will you be there for me?" she asks. It's an open question, but I notice her shiny green eyes lock intensely onto Arlo's.

After all this time, he's still in love with her.

"Always," he whispers.

"And what about Hope?" Dawn asks then, taking the joint from Arlo.

Faith sighs. "Hope is... different."

"How so?"

"Between juggling Beau and the business, teaching Hope our ways always fell by the wayside. Don't get me wrong, she's a strong activist against animal cruelty... and has never touched a slither of meat. She knows how disgusting and wrong the meat industry is."

"But she doesn't know about *our* work?" Arlo offers.

Suddenly, Faith's face drops into a deep, darkened frown. Whereas before, her face seemed just as flawless as always, now I can see the lines and creases marking her skin, exposing her true age. "That's not important," she replies stiffly. "All you need to concern yourselves with is Beau. Then I can focus on training Hope."

Dawn smirks, undeterred by Faith's less-than-impressed tone. "I think Daddy has taken a liking to your Hope."

A smile stretches out on Faith's face.

"I think so too," she replies.

Mischa

My heart stops. My lungs feel stiff, like lead cemented inside my chest.

"Misch… Misch, what ya doing?"

The sound of my boyfriend's voice rouses me from my stunned daydream, and I snap my head around to meet his concerned gaze. He sits in the driver's seat of his old banger of a car, one beefy hand poised over the gear stick, the other caressing the top of the steering wheel. He raises a dark eyebrow.

"I just can't believe I'm here," I gasp, instinctively clutching a hand to my chest.

At that, he smiles. He knows that he delivered.

"Is this the best birthday ever?" he grins, knowing full well that the answer is a definite, resounding *yes*.

"A million times yes," I whisper, lunging myself forward and burying my head in his chest. I inhale his familiar scent and grip onto his arms, trying to ground myself in this bizarre, real-life fantasy.

"Well, what are you waiting for?" he asks.

Nerves suddenly set in, like iron nails penetrating my skin. I can tell that he senses it because he suddenly takes hold of my upper arms and pushes me away so that I am at arm's length.

"Mischa Verity Parker," he says solemnly.

I groan.

"Listen. You are so, so worth this woman's time. She is going to see you, and she is going to instantly love you. Make no mistake. She's going to see how much effort you put into this meeting, and pair that with your adorable face and enchanting personality, she won't be able to let you out of her sight," Jace winks at me then.

My heart swells with love for him. How did I get so fucking lucky?

"But what if she doesn't?" I reply hoarsely. Just the mere thought of it is enough to splinter my heart.

"She will," he protests. "And if she doesn't, I want money for the petrol," he jokes.

I nudge him playfully in the ribs, and he leans over and pops open the car door on my side. "Now go on- out. Knock 'em dead," he says encouragingly.

Before I can open my mouth to protest, he's pushing me out of the door. "I'll come back in an hour," he says as I reluctantly slam the car door and poke my head in through the half-open window.

"Half an hour," I insist.

"No way," he smirks. "I love you."

A sigh filled with mixed emotions escapes my chest, and I return his smile. "I love you more."

"Impossible."

As soon as I have safely moved my head out of the way and taken a step backwards onto the pavement, his beat-up little car hurtles away, tyres screeching on the road. I tut and shake my head. My Jace might be the perfect man and the most amazing partner a girl could ever wish for, but a sensible driver he is *not*.

Slowly, I turn around and glance up at the huge house in front of me. It's right at the end of a very quiet, impressive-looking cul-de-sac full of huge, grand buildings fronted by vast, emerald green lawns. It's beautiful- and an entire universe away from the shitty bungalow that Jace and I share a few hours away.

Not that I mind living in a poky bungalow and driving around in a car that's seen better days. On the contrary, money doesn't mean a thing to me or us. That isn't why I'm here. Not by a long shot.

Faith Farmer.

She is the reason I am here.

Clearing my throat, I run my tongue along my lower lip. My mouth is as dry as the Sahara, and I'm paranoid that my trousers are creased. Maybe if Jace was still waiting beside me, I'd call the whole thing off.

I'd told him it was my dream to meet her, and it is. It's always been my dream to meet the woman who has practically led the revolution against animal cruelty. It's always been my dream to work with her alongside her. Shit, it's my dream to *be* her.

But she doesn't accept job applications or internships. She scouts out her employees. And after ten years of volunteering, taking courses, attending protests and demonstrations, I'd never even come close to even being merely noticed by her.

I'd tried to find her home address so many times, but every location I found always turned out to be a hoax. But I know that this one, the one that Jace tracked down, is the right one.

This is where *the* Faith Farmer lives.

My head spins.

I know that this is where she lives because I recognise the house, and the bushes, and the plants growing around the front of the house. I've practically memorised every inch of it from the photos in magazines.

I've no idea how Jace got a hold of the address, but I know that it wouldn't have been easy. How can I just back out of it now?

With a long, deep breath, I force my feet to move forwards. One in front of the other. There's no gate or tall iron railings. I guess the silent, tucked-away close is private enough, without the need for additional security. In a way, it's almost as though the place is embedded in its own kind of dense woodland, protected by happy and contented wildlife roaming freely amongst the trees and bushes.

Shoving the image of a brusque rejection towards the back of my mind, I speed up my movements, feigning fearlessness. It gets easier with every step as I fill my head with hopeful clouds of success.

What's the saying?

Don't focus on what could go wrong. Just think of what could go right.

Well, shit. If this goes right, it will change my entire life.

The money is the least of it, although it would be nice if Jace and I had a proper place to live, not some temporary shithole because I've dedicated my life to meeting Faith as opposed to getting some dead-end job to pay the bills.

I'm propelled forwards by my optimism, yet when I reach the marble steps leading up to a wide front porch exquisitely decorated in greenery, I pause. My nerves come flooding back all at once, my lungs filling, my stomach flipping. The skin up and down my arms prickles, and it occurs to me how fucking stupid I've been.

How many others before me had somehow managed to track down her house and just casually traipsed on down here as though they had a right? My cheeks flush with shame, and I go to turn around and jog back down the path, out of the luscious surroundings and back out onto the street.

But, it seems that fate has a different plan.

A shiver of electricity rushes down my spine as I rotate, and I'm suddenly aware of a pair of eyes upon me. I stop in my tracks and feel my throat turn uncomfortably dry and itchy.

Unable to move, I listen to the scratch of a metal lock turning, then the low creak of the front door behind me being pushed open.

"Hello?"

Her voice is different in real life. I've watched all of the interviews and television appearances. All of the televised charity work and documentaries. But in person, her voice is deeper, older. Still, there's no mistaking that it's her.

Like a timid animal caught in the headlights, I turn around in a flash, and a stunned gasp escapes my lips as I clasp my eyes on her.

Enchanting emerald green eyes pierce into me- not unpleasantly. Her irises shine with curiosity, conveying youth and energy that most people her age probably do not possess. Faith is standing in the doorway, one hand leaning up against the doorframe, as casual as anything as she considers me.

So many times, I have dreamed of or envisioned this moment. So many times, I have practised what I would say and do; how I would compose myself. However, typically, all of my carefully composed plans have deserted me, and I'm just standing there gawping like an invalid.

Finally, I force my lips to part. I attempt to make a noise.

But instead, everything goes black.

I feel a thump, and the noise rings in my eardrums.

Nothingness.

Hope

It's not long before the girl comes round. She can't be much older than me, and she's beautiful. Maybe a college student or a teenage runaway? She's got a short, dark brunette pixie-cut and delicate pointed features. Both of her ears are visible and studded with more earrings that can be counted at first glance.

Mum crouches down beside her and instructs me to get a cup of sweet, plant-based tea. It's the stuff that I suspect is infused with some kind of hallucinogenic and never touch as a result.

Once I've brought it back, the girl is awake, sitting almost upright, her lips trembling, and her eyes wide. I sigh as I kneel down to pass my mum the mug of hot liquid.

We've had a few of *these* before. Die-hard fans that stalk the internet for information about my mum. Usually hippies. How the hell they find out where we live, I don't know. I keep begging Mum to build a wall around the house or even get security guards, but she won't budge. She insists the system is good enough as it is and, in all fairness, so far it has been.

"I...I'm sorry," the girl mumbles, her cheeks turning a bright red. "Sorry for just turning up. I just..."

"Sssh," Mum smiles, handing her the mug. Without a single bat of an eyelid, the girl takes it and takes a generous gulp, as if my mum is a kindly nurse or an old family friend that she's known for years.

"What's your name?" I ask, unable to conceal the cold edge that tinges my voice. I can't help but feel annoyed that this girl had just chosen today of all days to pass out in front of our house. If Beau gets wind of it, who fucking knows how she'll react. And if she has one of her almighty kick-offs, what are the odds of our new 'staff' doing an immediate U-turn and sprinting for the hills? I shudder at the thought.

"Mischa," the girl musters, swallowing. The mug shakes in her dainty hand. She clears her throat, and she turns to my mother, clearly attempting to put on some sort of brave face. "I came here because I would really love a chance to interview for an internship… or an apprenticeship, or whatever really… even voluntary work I can do…" with every word, her voice wobbles more and more and eventually begins to crack. I find my irritation melting away.

Mum gestures for her to take another sip of her drink but doesn't say anything. When I look into the familiar creases of her face, I can tell that she is silently thinking. I couldn't explain or tell anyone about the process in which my mother goes about recruiting for the business. I've asked a few times, but my mum has an uncanny way of answering the question without truly answering it. All I know is that she doesn't adopt traditional methods of employing people. She scouts them out. Chooses them. And they always agree to her proposition. But still, on the few occasions where starstruck borderline stalkers have bowled up before, enquiring about job opportunities, my mother has never appeared to even give them a second thought.

Mischa finishes her brew, still sprawled on our front garden path, before Mother generously invites her in for a smoke. Of course, Mischa agrees. To be honest, she'd probably accept a crack pipe if my mum was offering it.

As she leads us through the house, I catch a glimpse of Beau playing in the living room with Dawn and D, seemingly delighted with her new playmates. She's so excitable, in fact, that she doesn't even notice our visitor. The puckered, deformed mounds of flesh that make up her face contort as she lets out a low bellow of laughter, jumping dangerously hard on one of the couches. Part of me feels a responsibility to go with them, but I'm overpowered, pulled by an intense curiosity to see what happens between my mum and Mischa. Besides, they *seem* to be getting on okay, no matter how weird it feels to me that a stranger could take to someone like my sister so quickly and with so little judgement or reservation.

In the kitchen, Mum lights up a spliff, and she shares it with Mischa, who quickly starts to loosen up. She tells us all about how passionate she is about animal rights and how she's followed all of my mum's work for as long as she can remember. We find out it's her birthday, and coming here was a treat arranged for her by her boyfriend.

My heart swells wistfully then.

Imagine having someone around to perform such romantic gestures? I stifle a humourless chuckle. *Yeah right.* Blood-splattered images of Mum's various mutilated conquests; body parts crushed and smeared all over the hallway flash through my mind like a horror movie. Boyfriends don't tend to fare well in our house. D is lucky that he's even lasted the first hour.

"Wow," smiles Mum. An amused flicker crosses her face, and for a moment, I think she's making fun of her. I feel a pang of sympathy, especially when I hear the excitement in Mischa's voice. But, as the girl continues babbling on, I'm stunned when Mum abruptly interjects with a sudden, "okay. I'll give you a job."

Mischa's eyes almost pop out of their sockets, and her full, peach-coloured lips part in amazement. "Wait… what?"

I raise an eyebrow at my mother expectantly, although I'm not all that surprised.

My mum is… a colourful character. Vibrant, electric, and full of surprises. She's so wildly unconventional, and yet it's like she can have whatever and whoever she wants at the drop of a hat.

Honestly, I don't know whether to admire her or to be suspicious of her. When I was a girl, I used to wonder if she was a witch. Somehow maintaining all this success; a squeaky clean public image complete with a following of do-gooders… yet also so fucking mysterious. So unpredictable. Full of surprises and tricks.

Like this, for example.

"Are you kidding me?" Mischa whispers.

Mum shakes her head, balances her spliff on the side of the ash tray, and holds out her arms. A whiff of her fruity scent mixed with smoke infiltrates my nostrils. Mischa gladly bundles herself into my mother's embrace and tears well up in her eyes.

I don't know whether to be proud or be sick.

"Oh my god…. oh my god…" giggles Mischa, manically. "Thank you so much, Faith, you won't regret this. I promise."

"I know I won't," Mum replies certainly, with a nod. "Honestly, I'm so humbled by your enthusiasm, and… well, I just couldn't *not* have you on my team."

Mischa is smiling so hard; I wonder if her face will break.

"You'll move in with us for the full training," my mum says.

Again, I'm surprised by this offer, but also not.

Like I say, my mother is full of surprises.

"Um…" Mischa's face drops into a frown of confusion as if she has misheard. "Move in with you?"

"You understand, we're a very close-knit community of workers at *Faithful Pharmaceuticals*," Mum says coolly, seamlessly, as if she delivers this speech on the regular. "You need to be on call due to the nature of scientific developments and such. It also includes extremely intense medical and biological training."

Mischa doesn't speak for a moment and turns to me as if for guidance. I remain straight-faced. I haven't a fucking clue what's going on.

"Unless you're unavailable…." Mum probes.

"No… no, I mean yes! I'm available. Of course, I am. This is my dream…." Mischa babbles quickly, "it's just… I kind of live in a bungalow with Jace…."

"He can visit whenever he likes," Mum says sweetly, "it's not a prison by any means." There's an underlying sharpness beneath her words.

The girl's face is twisted and uneasy. She doesn't know what to say or what to do. Clearly, this is a big decision, one that should not be taken lightly or made on the spot. Yet, she wants it so badly; she's afraid to say anything but yes.

Shuddering, I clutch my elbows and sense the gooseflesh that erupts out onto my skin. The atmosphere has dropped a few degrees. I run my tongue along my lower lip, cringed out by the awkward tension lingering between my mother and this perky teenager.

"Mischa, I really get good vibrations from you," Mum says, taking Mischa's hands in hers. "I do, and I always rely solely on my instincts, no matter how random or sporadic, don't I, Hope?" she turns to me.

Feebly, I nod because it's true.

"I'm susceptible to certain energies," Mum continues, "a gift which I credit all of my success to…."

Fucking hell.

But Mischa nods, her eyes glazing over as I watch her fall hopelessly in love with my weird hippy of a mother.

"And I feel strongly about you. But, I also sense that you are… maybe hesitant? What are you afraid of? You came here searching for a job, no? A way to help our cause?"

Swallowing, Mischa nods. I cannot help but feel a mixture of awe and repulsion as I watch my mother so effortlessly manipulate this girl. Play her like a fucking fiddle.

"I'm not afraid," Mischa says. "I just… it's just all happening so quickly, and I…."

Mum smiles and nods at her patiently. "Well, maybe sometime in the future, when you're absolutely certain…."

"I am," blurts out Mischa, interrupting her. "I am ready. Look, I was just a little surprised, is all. I expected I'd need to go through a bunch of interviews or something. I bet you have thousands of people wanting to work for you."

My mother lifts the joint again, purses it between her lips, and re-lights it. She takes it in her mouth and inhales, blowing out another milky white cloud of smoke that shrouds the area around her face.

"I tell you what," she says to Mischa. "I have friends visiting who are going to be helping out with my eldest daughter. I wanted to show them the lab. Would you like to join us? Get a feel for the work we are doing?"

At that, my brow furrows. The proposition smacks me hard across the face, and my fists involuntarily clench down by my sides. I'm furious.

Clearing my throat, I interrupt them. "What? But… you never let me go to the lab."

"You're too young, sweetheart," Mum tells me, shooting me a sympathetic glance. "It's illegal to allow a person under the age of eighteen to enter the premises."

Huffing, I roll my eyes, get up and stalk out of the room.

I resist the urge to remind my mother that it is very likely illegal to use the fucking bodies mutilated by my brain-damaged older sister for her little experiments. In fact, I'm pretty sure it constitutes covering up a murder. I highly doubt any policeman is going to come and be hung up on me going to my own mother's workplace.

This is bullshit.

For so long, I've badgered her about having a look round. I know for a fact that Beau has been on multiple occasions… now, she's offering to take a group of total randomers for a bloody tour?!

Unbelievable!

It's like there's a huge secret that I'm not allowed to be a part of.

This is bullshit.

Biting back tears of frustration, I stamp up the stairs to my bedroom. I slam the door behind me.

That'll show her. Not.

Pig

Faith is taking me, Mischa, Arlo, and Daddy to see the famous lab.

Faith's got one of those posh, shiny, oversized cars. It's a far cry from the grubby, rattling tin cans we are normally accustomed to travelling in. Or should I say *can*? Arlo had to sell the others. It was a vain, feeble attempt to crawl out of the dismal financial situation he'd spiralled into.

At first, it was okay. From what I've overheard in conversations and from fleeting glimpses of bank statements, Faith had left a huge sum of money. Really, it would have been enough to keep a household going for all this time, even if the businesses were only just breaking even.

But, without Faith, the place seemed to quickly turn into what me and my friends had originally thought it was all those years ago.

Just a party house full of carefree, suspiciously wealthy hippies.

All of the days blended into one intoxicated, drug-fuelled blur of chaos. And, after months of being forced to live in shit, chop up dead, rotting flesh, and witness death in its rawest, most horrific form time and time again, I let myself fall into addiction with the rest of them. It's funny because the day I first met Faith when she poached us from that country pub, I could barely even stomach a pint of beer. Within a year of her departure, I was guzzling down, snorting, or smoking anything I could get my hands on.

At first, Arlo would still force a group of us to go to the farm or the circus and keep shit moving along. But once we ran out of bodies, it became apparent that without Faith's... *ways of persuasion*, luring unsuspecting tourists home, drugging them, then subsequently torturing and killing them was a lot harder than anticipated.

As a result, the farm hasn't churned out a single can of dog food or blood-streaked breast milk in years. It has been years since the circus last put on a bloodthirsty showcase of poor innocents being ripped to shreds in front of a live audience.

Basically, Arlo has royally fucked everything. This is why I can't help but feel a tense knot of unease in my stomach every time I watch him lying to Faith's face about it. My heart pounds a little quicker, and I wonder when she will pounce on him and likely kill him with her own bare hands.

At least *I* can't be blamed. Personally, I'm thrilled that the farm and the circus are out of business. Unlike the sadistic psychopaths I live with, I see the torture and murder for what it really is. It's not 'God's work' or 'karma,' as Faith says.

It's absolutely diabolical.

We pull up at a petrol station, and Faith nods at me, signalling that I should get out and fill up the tank. With a low sigh, I oblige. As I'm exiting the vehicle, she starts chatting to Mischa, the new girl. Part of me wants to scream in the girl's face to run for the hills, but I know that would put us both in danger.

I feel Arlo watching me from the passenger side of the car, subtly, just out of the corner of his eye. Whilst I'm filling the car, I glance around and note the people all around us. There's even a policeman sitting in an unmarked car just a few metres away. In my head, I envision dropping the petrol pump, sprinting across the forecourt, and calmly explaining that I was kidnapped sixteen years ago by the people in the car.

It would be so easy.

Escaping their hold would be easy. I've gained their trust. I'm allowed to do certain things independently. I'm allowed to make trips into town, handle knives, and walk about the house freely.

But there's something deeper than physical restraints that keep me tied to them. Maybe it's the easy access to the drugs and the comfortable life they've provided for me. It's easy to forget the horrifying conditions I used to live under and the stomach-curdling things they made me see and do. Even to overlook the fact that they brutally killed the love of my life, took photos, and pasted them up in my grimy, minuscule cell, so her death was the first thing I saw each morning when I opened my eyes.

All of it, somehow buried deep in the back of my head, locked tightly away beneath layer upon layer of denial, brainwashing, and the fuzz of the drugs.

Because when I'm curled up in one of the lavish, upholstered sofas, so high that I feel like I am floating, I forget all the bad shit.

How can a sane person forget that? Be desensitised to it, even? Click.

The shrill clip of the tank indicating its fullness pulls me from my daze. When I drop my stare, I note Arlo looking at me sharply through the window. Hurriedly, I close the car up again, replace the pump and then tap the pay-at-pump point with Arlo's bank card.

As I get back in the car, I do not give the policeman a second look.

Unsurprisingly, the lab is a fair distance away from the house. As the car speeds along increasingly rural roads; and the dense fields and greenery grow thicker and thicker, I see that Faith has taken her usual initiative and built her business as far out in the sticks as possible. My stomach fills with dread as light-hearted chatter fills the car, as if we are the average nuclear family on a road trip, as opposed to on our way to a place that I'm certain will be filled with typically nasty surprises.

I even sense nervousness in Arlo's laughter, and D squirm uneasily in his seat. I'd always assumed that Arlo's killer instinct would be a constant part of his persona, but I suppose all the drugs have softened his previously sharpened edges. If it wasn't for the horrific images permanently branded into my skull, maybe I'd find it difficult to believe that he used to be a ruthless, bloodthirsty monster.

Faith's lab is, similarly to the farm, and the circus, an inconspicuous-looking building, dark brown and so dreary that it almost blends in with the countryside surrounding it.

"Oh…" Mischa says, confused.

"Hm?" Faith's sparkling emerald eyes flit upwards to the rear view mirror, where she fixes the girl with an expectant glance.

Mischa's cheeks burn red, and she stumbles nervously over her words. "Nothing… I just… this looks different to the pictures in the magazine."

Chuckling, Faith indicates and swerves into the wide, long space in front of the building. "There's more than one lab," she says.

Something lurches in my chest as her worlds hang chillingly in the air. *Of course, there's more than one lab.* No doubt this is the unregulated lab, the one she hides from the tax man, the authorities, and the public because of whatever dark and evil things are happening inside it.

"I always just assumed the one in London was the main headquarters," Mischa says.

"That's the headquarters, that's where we deal with the campaigns, charities, the PR, and the business side of things," explains Faith, tucking the car neatly into a space conveniently concealed by dark green shrubs. "I don't want my scientists and researchers being distracted by the hustle and bustle of the city. It's much more productive for them to be out here…" she shut off the car and turned around her seat to flash Mischa a wide smile.

Mischa blinks and looks around at the seemingly deserted forecourt of the house. Before she can open her mouth and ask the question that surely must be scorching everyone's tongues, Faith opens up her car door and slams it quickly behind her.

"There's probably staff parking out back or something," D offers with a shrug.

I shiver and stop myself from telling him how much I doubted it.

Mischa

I feel cold as Faith leads us across the land towards the small, subtle doorway at the side of the lab. The sky has suddenly darkened, and wisps of grey float together above us. A low rumble of wind blows against my neck, making all of the little hairs stand up on end.

I'm going to THE lab. I've landed my dream job.

In a matter of hours, my entire life has changed.

I should be bouncing off the walls with excitement as I trail after my new employer into a dark, windowless corridor that smells faintly of chlorine.

But my gut stirs. My senses prickle.

I remember the saying *when something seems too good to be true, it usually is*. This doesn't happen in real life, least of all to somebody like me.

So why has it?

I can't shake the feeling that I need to put up my defences and not allow myself to become entirely comfortable. Who knows what will happen next?

Inside, I scold myself for being so pessimistic. I tell myself that if I walk around with a face like a smacked arse, surely Faith or one of the others will notice, and that'll be that. They'll drop me for lack of enthusiasm, just as quickly as I got picked up.

Faith flicks on a light that is just a little brighter than the dusky air. Once the front door has closed behind us, it feels like the dead of night. The air is hot and moist, like in a rainforest.

At the end of the passage, Faith stops in front of the four of us. There's me, Arlo, D, and the timid Indian man called Phoenix. The three of them seem confident, as though Faith is their queen, and they've been given the honour of escorting her to her throne.

"Now, before we go in," Faith says, widening her eyes to emphasise the seriousness of her words. "All rooms are soundproof. This is because it is vital that silence is maintained from visitors. You must remain quiet; otherwise, you could potentially distract one of the scientists, resulting in error or injury...."

I nod in understanding.

"Secondly," Faith continues, "some of my research methods are... somewhat unorthodox."

At that, I laugh, thinking she is being sarcastic about all of the companies that still believe hurting and killing innocent animals in the name of science is acceptable.

"However, I'd ask you to not be alarmed or ask questions about whatever you see. Everything is perfectly safe and morally acceptable. At the end of our walk around, I can answer any questions you may have."

Odd choice of words. But I shrug it off. It's true that the weirdest, most eccentric people are usually also the most brilliant.

"Last of all, please do not touch anything," Faith says with a smile. "We wouldn't want to contaminate any studies or samples."

A reasonable request. Another murmur of agreement passes through our tour group, and Faith guides us further up the corridor until she reaches a heavy, bolted door. She taps in a code so impossibly quickly that I can't make out even a single digit, then presses a finger onto a scanner. The bolts and locks creak open then, the metal scraping loudly as it clicks out of place, and the door is cleanly released from its iron hinge.

Immediately, a bright, greyish light from the room within spills into the hall, illuminating the gloomy passage where we all stand.

"After you," says Faith brightly, pressing her back up against the door and gesturing for us to enter.

Arlo goes first, taking long, masculine strides as if to assert his position as the oldest male. Phoenix and D nod for me to go ahead of them and wait politely whilst I turn to face the open doorway and purposefully follow Arlo through.

The first area we get to is disappointingly small, like a little grey cube. There are metal elevator doors embedded into the wall on one side, and on the other, there is a decrepit-looking shutter with plastic flaps guarding the top. To my surprise, Arlo does not wait in front of the shutters but instead walks straight through them as though he owns the place. I glance uncertainly back at Faith, but she nods encouragingly but then reminds me to stay quiet by holding up a finger to her lips.

As I slip through the sweating plastic flaps into the second room, the first thing that hits me is the smell. The stench is so pungent that it actually stops me in my tracks, and I find that bile begins to crawl up into my throat. Rooted to the spot, my face involuntarily contorts with disgust as I scan the white-painted space for the source of the ungodly odour.

But the room, and all of those who occupy it, seem remarkably ordinary. There are about eight different work tops, two of which are occupied by two people in lab coats and protective eyewear. One of them, a young girl, I notice, has Down's syndrome. As we enter the room, she glances up, smiles, and waves at us. The other scientist is rummaging through a metal trolley containing various liquids and potions in glass tubes and bottles. She doesn't bat an eyelid at our arrival.

"Hi," I smile at the girl with Down's, enchanted by her sweet, innocent smile and the enthusiasm glistening in her irises. I suddenly feel completely ridiculous for being suspicious of Faith. How could anyone feel unease around an employer who not only is a fierce animal rights advocate but also makes a point of hiring people with special needs and disabilities?

Arlo whirls around and shoots me a sharp glare that feels like the tip of a blade slashing through my skin. I shudder and remember Faith's rules. *No talking or making any noise.*

I give Arlo an apologetic smile before avoiding his eye. Instead, I tread gently around the outer corner of the room until I am beside the two workers at the desk. Stretched out in front of them, on a kind of light projector, is a strange, brownish material, with an ugly bubble of puss and rash across its centre. I stifle a disgusted grimace. I see that they are using the chemicals in the trolley to mix a new concoction in a separate beaker and apparently testing it out on the gruesome-looking wound.

Wrinkling my nose, I wonder what Faith has used as a substitute for animal hides. Upon closer inspection, I see that the rash is weeping as if it's an actual, real wound on a living creature. It also smells just like an actual, real wound on a living creature.

When I finally tear my eyes away from the grim scene, I look over at the opposite wall in the far corner of the room. I cock my head and squint my eyes in confusion, then carefully step closer to inspect a kind of three-tier clothesline strung out across the wall.

More sheets of artificial skin hang there limply, each one encrusted with a different kind of ailment.

One has a huge, black growth protruding from it, whilst another is covered in a spattering of tiny red pinpricks. But the worst, by far, is one with three neat slashes across the middle, each one leaking a disgusting yellow trickle of slimy liquid. I clamp my hand to my mouth as more bile threatens the back of my throat.

I feel a hand on my shoulder and see that Faith is standing behind me. She looks concerned, and for a moment, I worry she thinks that I am not up to the job. Quickly, I force a wide smile and offer a thumbs up, signalling that artificial wounds are totally my bag. At that, she smiles back and gestures for me to lead through to the next chamber. I try not to look too enthusiastic.

There's another opening with the same grimy plastic flaps, and I'm disappointed to find that the horrific stench still mercilessly attacks each of my nostrils as I push through them.

But I'm quickly distracted from the pungent odour.

My heart stops. My jaw falls open as I take in the room with wide-eyed horror.

I freeze.

Mischa

It's smaller than the other room. The floor is tiled, like the kind you find in the changing rooms at swimming pools. There are even drains across each wall, and disgusting swirls of dark brown slowly ooze through their metal grates. But that's not what makes the hair on the back of my neck stand up.

Goose flesh breaks out across every inch of my body, and I feel my blood chill as I set eyes on the operating table in the centre of the room. Just like in a real surgery, there are large metal lights blaring down at the lifeless hunk of... whatever it is on the table.

I tell myself that it can't possibly be real.

It's just that it looks so... real.

Faith puts her hand in the small of my back, and I force myself to take a few more steps forward.

Three figures dressed in blue scrubs, wearing surgical masks and gloves, are gathered around what appears to be a naked man, lying unconscious beneath the spotlights. His face is gaunt and shimmers with a yellowish tinge to his skin. At the other end of his body, his left leg has been amputated.

Not just amputated- it looks as though the limb has been brutally hacked off. A chaotic mass of deep red wires and shredded muscle spill out, saturating the bed, dripping like wine onto the tiled floor.

I smack a hand over my lips and involuntarily hunch over, terrified that I'll be the one to vomit all over the place.

I scold myself.

Obviously, it's not fucking real.

With clenched teeth, I force my eyes open and stare at the gore, ignoring the thick, despicable stench that overpowers my senses. One of the surgeons bends down and places their hands inside a tall, metal ice box by their side. They pull a clean, rubbery-looking artificial limb from the container, arms quivering slightly underneath its weight. I glance to my right to see that the others are all just as transfixed. None of them look quite as shocked or repulsed as I feel.

I turn back and watch with curled toes as they place the leg onto the table like dropping meat on a slab. I remember reading about this somewhere before that Faith's company was in the process of researching prosthetic limbs for amputees that would be surgically attached and fully functional. For a moment, the excitement squirming in my belly eradicates the disgusting taste at the back of my throat. Working here would be witnessing miracles every day. Life-changing miracles that will change the world for the better ten times over…

Alas, the blast of cheeriness in my system is quashed just as quickly as it appears.

One of the surgeons presses a plastic mask over the dummy's mouth, whilst the others work quickly together to secure straps across its torso.

To my horror, the dummy coughs and splutters. Its eyelids flutter open, revealing bloodshot, yellowing whites and crazed pupils that flit manically around. When the surgeon removes the mask, the dummy coughs even louder, as if it's trying to speak, but it is choking on air.

Open-mouthed, I glance at Faith, but she isn't looking at me. None of the others are. Each of them displays unreadable expressions, watching the terrifying scene play out with not so much as the bat of an eyelid.

"W-w-w-what are you doing?" the dummy finally rasps, its lips now covered in phlegm and spit from all the coughing. The head jerks up as the surgeons continue to silently work, preparing materials on a metal dish.

At the sight of the bloody stump of a leg, the dummy's mouth gapes, and his eyeballs bulge from their sockets. He lets out a deafening scream which pierces my eardrums like a knife slicing through flesh.

"AAAHHHH!" he screeches. His neck thrashes from left to right, but the rest of his body is tightly bound to the table beneath him. "SOMEBODY HELP ME!"

I clamp down hard on the insides of my mouth, my palms sweating as the sound of his agonised shrieks plague my head and chill me to the core. It sounds so painfully real. It's taking every cell of effort in my body not to do something.

Why would an artificial dummy, or even a robot, need to cry for help? I open my mouth to ask but then close it again.

I don't want to sound foolish.

The man... *the dummy*... begins sobbing.

It's harrowing to watch a fully grown male cry and scream like a tiny newborn, his face all crumpled up, bright red with despair.

If the robot has the same effect on the surgeons as it does on me, they do a good job of not showing it. They act like he isn't there and simply gets on with positioning the prosthetic limb against the dummy's bloody, weeping stump.

My stomach turns as I watch one of them pick up a huge needle loaded with a thick, strong-looking black thread. With not a great deal of precision, the masked worker plunges it straight into the edge of the blood-soaked jungle where the man's leg should be.

He screeches.

The surgeon ignores him and instead tugs the needle roughly through the skin, causing fresh, bright red blood to sprout from the puncture.

Mesmerised by the horror of it, I remain rooted still to the spot, my mouth agape and my eyes wide as the so-called professional crudely stitches the prosthetic limb onto the man's quivering amputation.

I realise that sweat has poured from my skin, and my t-shirt is sticking to my back.

I'm cold.

I shiver.

A warm hand on my shoulder breaks me out of the spell, and I startle, snapping my head to the right to see Faith smiling at me and gesturing for me to go onto the next room. Wordlessly, I oblige, forcing one foot in front of the other as I trail around the operating table and attempt to avoid the grotesque, bloody trails that are swirling around the tiles.

Dread congeals in the pit of my stomach.

Stop being so fucking stupid, I scold myself. This is science. Cruelty-free science. It's my dream job. I can't show myself up just because I'm too much of a pussy to deal with a bit of fake blood.

Nevertheless, I'm grateful to finally get out of the room.

The smell isn't as bad as I step through the doorway into a pale blue corridor. Once we're all in, Faith slides across a door and cuts off the echoing screams of the fake amputee.

I look down the passage and note that ahead there are eight identical doors, four on each side. It reminds me of a corridor in a school.

"We can talk quietly for the moment," Faith says in a low, calm voice.

I debate asking what the fuck that last room was about, but I hold my tongue out of fear of sounding like an idiot.

"So what we've seen so far is one of the testing areas, and then the theatre," Faith explains. "Testing area one is where we test different solutions and remedies on skin wounds, rashes, and other superficial ailments," she smiles proudly, "in fact, that was the room where we discovered the cure for all types of eczema and psoriasis."

"There are many other testing areas, each one used for a different purpose. For example, testing area 2 is used purely for testing the safety of my fragrances and cosmetics. Testing area 3 is used to identify the safety and any potential side effects of medications…."

"How…" I chime in, desperate to ask how these can be tested so efficiently without live animals. But Faith cuts me off, either not wanting to answer my question or not registering that I had spoken.

"We also have multiple theatres, although they are all equipped to facilitate a range of different procedures and experiments. Just now, you saw one of many of our latest attempts at inventing a fully functioning, surgically attached limb," pride washes across her face, and her pretty green eyes light up with excitement. "We're so close now. We've already secured a final prototype for cows, but…."

Suddenly, a deafening siren screams through the building, slashing through Faith's sentence and abruptly cutting her off.

Pig

Even Faith is stunned by the sudden eruption of noise. Her face momentarily collapses into a stunned sinkhole, betraying her true emotions; however, she quickly shakes it off and resumes her calm demeanour.

"Relax, guys, I'm sure it's a false alarm," Faith says, although her words are barely even audible over all of the din. There is a heavy clang of metal. She freezes.

I stifle a laugh. Never, in all my years, did I ever think I would see the day. Maybe it's an age thing. Is the impenetrable Faith afraid? Shit, I feel as though I am in an alternate universe.

Arlo and Faith exchange a glance. A silent conversation, a mutual understanding passing from one to the other. He nods at Daddy, then at me, although I'm unsure what the gesture means. Unfortunately, it all becomes apparent just moments later when one of the doors down the corridor creaks open, and a slight, stick-like figure suddenly spills through the gap in the door.

"HELP!"

It's a woman. She races on wobbly, painfully skinny legs which are completely bare, apart from the grotesque slashes of dark crimson that stain her pale skin. "HELP ME!" her voice croaks, every syllable ricocheting around the passage.

I feel Arlo tense beside me, ready to pounce. But apparently, he's out of practise, and the girl is so desperate, so full of torment, and fuelled by torture-induced madness that she is too fast for him. She speeds past our group. As she passes, my jaw drops. The girl, beneath all of the wounds and bruises, is so painfully thin you can see the outline of every single ridge of her skeleton beneath her skin. Clumps of her hair are missing, exposing her white scalp beneath, the rest of it sticking up in chaotic tufts of matted fluff.

"After her," Faith snarls, loud enough to hear this time. Obedient as ever, Arlo lunges after the girl down another passage.

"Faith..." Mischa is stunned. She looks pleadingly at her, her wide eyes begging for some kind of logical explanation.

But there's no time for it. Behind her, several more of the doors have been pushed open. Out of one comes a tall man, every inch of his skin a nasty shade of bright scarlet red. As he pounds down the hall, a harrowing screech of agony flowing from his throat, I see that the redness is a putrid mash of raw flesh and scraps of leftover skin, sodden with blood. Before I can stop myself, the bile is in my throat, and I hunch over, vomiting all over my shoes.

"Get them," Faith barks at Daddy, who suddenly does not look so confident. But he forces himself. He was born into this, but up until now, the stories of violence and brutality were all nothing but stories. Now, he's been flung right into the deep end.

Retching, I force myself to look up. Daddy rugby tackles the skinned man to the ground with ease. They struggle on the floor. Besides them, I see another man crawling slowly down the passage towards them. Apart from bright red scars around his wrists, and two lumpy, lifeless cylinders where his legs should be, he looks almost unscathed. He stops behind Daddy and lunges forward, clamping the boy's head between his big, beefy hands.

"HELP!" screeches Daddy, his boyish face crumpling pathetically as soon as the movement takes him by surprise. He lets go of the skinless man and thrashes about on the ground as if he is being attacked by flesh-eating zombies as opposed to two mutilated prisoners.

"Pig," Faith hits me hard, the side of her hand sharply jabbing me in the back of the neck. She forgets to call me by my fake name. "Move. Now. Get them back in their cells."

At that, Mischa swirls around her mouth agape with horror. I ignore her, knowing what the consequences will be if I do not immediately follow Faith's instructions.

You see, even after all this time, it's still ingrained in me. It's still branded into my brain, permanently scarred across my skull that no matter what, if Faith doesn't get what she wants, extremely bad shit happens.

Usually, to me.

I force myself to move towards them, but I hesitate when I'm a metre away. Another door opens then, revealing a slow-moving ghost of a woman whose face is saturated in such despair that it makes my heart sink. She doesn't attempt to run, just shuffles forwards. A horrified gasp escapes my lips as I see the battered and bloodied stumps where her shoulders should be. A blood and puss-soaked bandage dangles feebly from one of the wounds, no doubt the shoddy work of one of the so-called surgeons. My stomach churns, threatening to empty its contents once again.

"FUCK!" I'm torn from my stunned daze when the sharp pierce of teeth sinks into the flesh on my ankle. "FUCK!" I scream again as the shock sends me teetering over like a great tree being chopped down. The side of my skull collides with the hard floor with an almighty smack, and pain floods my senses.

It's the guy on the floor, crawling over me with such concentration on his face that in spite of my injury, I almost find myself rooting for him. Daddy continues to wrestle the skinned man whilst another hysterical girl appears from behind one of the other doors. This one is covered in horrific, bulbous sores in sickly shades of green and yellow, each one weeping a foul-smelling liquid that signifies a nasty infection. The revolting rash covers every inch of her flesh, even her bald head, but she is surprisingly speedy as she dashes across us down the passage.

Her sprint is short-lived.

BANG.

An ear-shattering crack slices through the air, and the girl flies backward onto the ground.

BANG.

BANG.

BANG.

One by one, the tortured souls down the corridor flop down like dominoes, landing in a hopeless heap all around Daddy and me, creating a wreath of death and suffering. The young man and I stare at each other with a mixture of shock and terror.

Shock at the bloody, gruesome circumstances we find ourselves buried in and terror at the prospect of facing Faith.

Even Daddy, who has never witnessed Faith's wrath firsthand, looks as though he is about to shit himself.

The siren is cut off mid-wail, and the blood-splattered corridor is plunged into silence.

I force myself to turn. Mischa is on her knees, her head buried in her hands. One of the faceless surgeons is standing beside Faith, a gun poised in his gloved hands.

Faith's brow is furrowed deeply, her face bright red.

My heart sinks.

Not for the first time in my life since that catastrophic evening where I was captured and dragged into Faith's shitstorm of an orbit, I ask myself if this will finally be the end.

Hope

I can't help but feel uneasy. The house seems so eerily quiet with Mum gone, even though Beau is still here, crashing around and making a racket as always. The sense of emptiness is only amplified by the lingering presence of Dawn, the skinny woman with the gaunt face and questionable eyes. More than anything, I want to flee upstairs to my bedroom, but something nags at me not to leave Beau with a stranger.

Mum's old friend or not, Beau would snap the woman like a twig with one finger if anything were to trigger her. And I'm in *no* mood to be cleaning up another dead body anytime soon.

"So, Hope," Dawn says suddenly, breaking the crisp quiet that hangs between us. I keep my eyes focused on the television screen hanging on the wall, mindless cartoons dancing across the picture. "I bet you're the envy of all your friends."

In response, I let out a brief grunt. Truthfully, I *am* the envy of all of my friends, but that doesn't mean I'm not still pissed off about not being able to go on a tour of the lab.

"There's no other mother like yours," she continues in a weird, hazy voice.

"What, do you fancy her or something?" I smirk sarcastically, finally turning to face her. Instantly, I regret making the snarky comment because Dawn's eyes are deathly cold, shooting rigged blades in my direction without a single sound. Her fragile, skinny body is curled up on the opposite end of the couch; bony limbs tucked up underneath her. "Sorry," I find myself muttering pathetically.

"That's quite alright, Hope," Dawn says without missing a beat, her voice bright, a sickly smile plastered onto her face. "I understand how odd this must be for you. Us all suddenly turning up here, your mother just letting us in. Trusting us so easily when I'm sure you've never seen her trust anybody else."

My heart beats in my chest as I absorb her words. She's right. Of course, she is. Who wouldn't be suspicious and confused about all of this? Before I can stop myself, my indignation is pouring from my lips.

"She's so secretive about the lab," I blurt out. "Obviously, I know she earns a lot of money, and she does good work, but other than that, I know pretty much nothing. She doesn't give anything away."

Dawn continues to smile. "Why do you think that is?"

"Well, I don't know," I retort defensively, "it's not like I can't keep secrets. I mean…" I cut myself short then, frowning in frustration at myself for almost spilling the beans. I glance across the room at Beau, who is staring aimlessly out of a window, her lumpy forehead pressed up to the cold glass.

"It's okay," Dawn says with a nod, beady eyes gleaming. "I know about Beau's… habits."

"You do?" I ask curiously.

"Your mother couldn't very well ask us to come here and help without telling us what we're dealing with, could she?"

There's something marginally comforting about knowing that somebody else knows about my sister. To know that that same person isn't hot-footing it straight down to the local mental asylum or police station. Maybe Beau isn't as fucked up as I thought. I briefly consider telling Dawn about how Mum uses the… remains… as extra subjects at her lab. But in the end, I don't. It's impossible to tell where the line is, separating every detail from okay and not okay. Any moment now, I keep warning myself, I'll say something that takes it too far, and we'll all be in hot water.

"It's alright," Dawn says as if she can read my mind. "I owe my life to your mother. I'll forever be in her debt and will therefore always be in her service. And that also means yours."

"Arlo and Phoenix, too?"

Dawn nods, "every last one of us. There's a lot of us back at the old place. We're a family."

An amused snigger comes from my mouth at that, "you mean like a cult? Like the Manson's or something?"

"Pretty much," Dawn continues to smile, although she does not laugh or even remotely appear to be joking. "Your mother is one in a million. I truly mean that. So many people would never have seen the light had it not been for her."

"You mean about animals?" I ask. "That's kind of my mum's bag. I feel like she loves animals more than she loves humans."

Dawn licks her lips, briefly revealing the broken and yellowing tombstone teeth that take up her mouth. "Animals are superior to humans," she tells me solemnly, "by way of innocence. Animals are never cruel or evil. They simply act on instinct. And it was that way of thinking that helped me to realise I needed to stop whoring myself out and filling my veins with poisonous shit. It was that realisation that made me see the truth and that my life was pointless if I wasn't using it to do important work."

A cold shiver of electricity zaps down my spine. She sounds so rehearsed and sombre as if the words are branded or tattooed onto her very soul. I look away from her and stare across the room at Beau, who is still in the same stationary position, gazing out at the garden.

"Beau, you okay?" I ask, more to end this strange, unnerving conversation with Dawn rather than out of concern. Beau ignores me, as she often does when she is in one of her trances, but I sense Dawn shuffling closer to me on the sofa out of the corner of my eye. My head snaps to the side, and my pupils meet hers.

"I can answer your questions, you know," Dawn tells me in a hoarse, barely audible whisper.

My skin prickles, and I attempt to swallow as the back of my throat dries. "What do you mean?"

The woman scuttles further towards me like some kind of human-sized insect, hunger gleaming in her eyes. I resist the urge to shrink back against the sofa cushions, determined not to show any kind of fear or weakness.

"There are lots of secrets in your mum's past," Dawn purrs. "Things she doesn't want you to know about."

I feel my eyebrow arch, "I thought you just said you owe her your life. And now you're basically slagging her off?"

Dawn's smile does not falter. Instead, her grotesque, sagging face comes closer to mine. I involuntarily inhale the stale stench of cigarette smoke protruding from her lips.

"Not slagging her off. I don't know why she keeps these secrets," she shrugs. "It's most unlike her. I'm very surprised she hasn't told you the truth."

As much as my dislike for the woman intensifies, I can't help but feel curiosity burn inside my soul. "Well, come on then, what is it? What do you want to tell me?"

"£150," Dawn says simply.

I frown and fold my arms. "Sorry?"

"That's the price. I'll tell you everything. Right from the very beginning."

"Why do you need that? My mum's paying you," I get up then, unable to stand her any longer. "I don't know what the fuck is up with you, but you're a fucking freak."

The old hag continues to smile, "maybe so. But there are certain things your mother will never tell you. And your only hope of discovering the truth is through me."

"You wait till I tell my mum about this," I snap. "Who the hell do you think you are?"

Dawn laughs, throwing her head back.

"More to the point, who the hell do you think you are? Do you know who your father is? I doubt it. You don't even know your own mother."

My heart stops in my chest for a moment. I clench my fists to find that my palms are sweaty and hot. That uncomfortable feeling of insecurity rears its ugly head. Every moment and every action of my mothers that ever made me feel like I never really knew her at all hits me at once like a ton of falling bricks.

"Why shouldn't I just go and ask my mum?" I whisper, already knowing the answer.

"She'll never tell you," says Dawn matter-of-factly, glancing down at her filthy, stubby nail beds.

"Not until you prove that you're one of us."

Mischa

When we finally leave the lab, my entire body is drenched in a cold sweat. I dither along behind the rest of the group, every inch of me shaking and shuddering, the bloody scene that I've just witnessed now permanently etched at the front of my brain. Every time I close my eyes, even for the briefest of moments, the image of gore flashes up in my head. The dead, defenceless bodies of those... *patients*? People? Humans? *Subjects?* Blood and bone exploding with each cruel, merciless gunshot.

My ears still ring, throbbing with the painful echo of the deafening noise.

As we reach the car, Faith turns towards me, roughly grabbing my arm so that I'm forced to move away from the rest of the group with her.

"I'm sorry you had to see that without any warning," she tells me in a hushed tone, her entrancing green eyes twinkling as they bore into my soul.

My teeth chatter. "I-i-i-is that normal?" I can just about muster, my body aching with dread as I consider the grim possibility that this is not the first time so much blood has been shed in Faith's lab. "I just... I thought your procedures were about... cruelty-free...."

Her face sharpens, and the grip of her fingers tightens around my flesh. I feel tears ebbing in my eyes and realise I'm trembling with fear. Immediately, she releases me and embraces me in her arms.

The floodgates open, and I find myself sobbing like a child into the space between her shoulder and neck.

"Oh darling, oh darling, I'm so sorry," Faith mutters into my ear, her breath tickling my cheek. The warmth of her tongue does strange and magical things to me, and I feel my entire body quiver with something so overpowering that for a moment, I forget my terror. The horrific images I witnessed within the walls of the lab, just like that, are drowned out by her comforting mumblings, slowly numbing me to the tremors that course through my veins.

"It isn't what it appears," Faith tells me, pushing me away from her so that I am at arms' length all of a sudden, and her pretty face is back in my vision. "I know it looks to be darker and more vicious than it actually is, which is why I am so particular about who I employ."

At that, my skin prickles. I can't help but perk up at the idea of winning her approval. I wonder if she can sense the pathetic excitement which must radiate off of me like a morning sun beam.

"Why me?" I hear myself ask in a short, breathless gasp.

Faith smiles and rubs my shoulder with the pad of her thumb, "how about we get back and talk about this properly?" she nods behind me at the darkening sky, "it'll be getting chilly soon. And it's time for dinner."

And for some reason, that's all it takes. Just a moment ago, I was shaking like a leaf, genuinely fearing that I'd become one of those stupid girls that unknowingly walks straight into the crazed psychopath's trap. Now, the spring is back in my step as I toddle along behind Faith as if I'm a puppy scurrying behind its new master.

Just like in all of her photos, in all the news articles and videos, the strange, invisible pull that seems to connect us only strengthens. I find myself infatuated by her. Hopelessly hypnotized by her.

As I traipse willingly into the back of her car and melt back into the atmosphere, tuning in and out of the hum of conversation going on around me, I attempt to reason.

Faith, this woman, my *idol*, is a world-renown celebrity. Her name is splashed on every wall of beauty stores and pharmacies; her potions featured a million times over on seemingly every platform. Whatever it was in the lab that just happened, it can't be anything too sordid. Famous, successful people who do good things for animals and the environment can't do any wrong.

Not when they're constantly bathed in so much lime light.

Not without being caught and losing everything.

I allow myself to settle back against the luxurious leather of the car seat and a long, deep breath.

Everything is going to be fine.

Pig

I notice at the dinner table later that evening that the events that took place at the lab earlier have been seamlessly glossed over. Whilst none of us are exactly strangers to watching living things suffer and die an ultimately brutal, agonising death, it's been a long while since the farm and the circus were anything like what they used to be.

It's been a long while since I actually *saw* somebody be killed.

Arlo and some of the other guys from the family like to brag about it enough, but I've always suspected it's some kind of front. If they were really producing enough meat and putting on enough sick, sadistic shows in the big top, they'd surely need help from a pathetic prisoner. A pathetic prisoner like me, who's somehow become institutionalised by the same cult that tore his life into shit.

But no, there's no mention of blood stains, kidnap, or death around this dinner table. Just light-hearted chatter between old friends, with Faith letting out her irritatingly infectious hoots of laughter at regular intervals. Like vultures, Dawn and Arlo hang on to her every word, responding to every quip and question as though they worship the ground she walks on. Meanwhile, Daddy and Hope flirt over a bowl of bread, and Beau dribbles soup all over her deformed lips and jaw.

If it wasn't for the glass bongs lining the table runner, maybe an outsider would even think it's just a normal family dinner.

Or maybe, even, if it wasn't for the increasing amount of loud, distressed-sounding sniffles coming from Dawn.

I force myself to look up at her just as she wipes a fresh sheen of sweat from her forehead. I grimace, a foul taste burning the back of my throat, and I glance over at Faith, who is watching Dawn intently with those bright, emerald green eyes. That familiar glint dancing within her iris matches the one that still, to this day, haunts my dreams.

"Are you okay, Dawn?" Faith asks, putting down her fork and reaching for her crimson black glass of wine. She lifts it to her lips and sips. It looks like blood. "You're looking a little peaky."

The low chatter at the table silences then, and I sense everybody's gaze flit over to Dawn. Even Beau.

"I've never been better," smiles Dawn, getting up from the table. "I'm just going to the bathroom." Immediately, she heads towards the wide archway in the dining room that leads back to the wide staircase leading up to the bedrooms.

"Why not go to the toilet down here?" Faith asks, causing Dawn to stop dead in her tracks. I suppress a cold shiver when I hear the sliver of ice in her tone.

Dawn breathes out and turns back to face Faith. She's looking worse and worse by the minute. The withdrawals are clearly messing her up from the inside in a bad way.

"Women's problems," Dawn says with a forced smile. Her crusty knuckles clench down by her sides. "I'd like a bit of privacy."

Then, Faith stands up. She puts down her wine glass onto the dining table with a hard clatter. The sound slashes through the tension in the room like a bolt of lightning. Beau growls like a threatened dog and bears her stained, glistening teeth. Suddenly, my appetite is gone.

"I have any sanitary products you might need in the downstairs bathroom," Faith replies patiently, her lip curling upwards, words leaking from her lips in a passive-aggressive drawl. "And it's down the hall, so you won't be disturbed."

"Mum, what the hell?" Hope's voice startles me, just as much as it startles Arlo, Dawn, and Daddy. Her pretty face is scrunched up into an indignant frown as she stares at her mother, "let the woman go to the toilet, Christ."

Mischa looks like she has something to say too, but she holds her tongue. Her eyes are wide with a mixture of alarm and awe. I'm not surprised. I should be amazed that she's even still here after earlier. Then again, it's not like running away is even a choice where Faith is involved. If she wants you, she has you.

And if she can't have you, you *die*.

"Why don't you cut the shit, Dawn?" Faith asks, ignoring both of her daughters, never dropping the sickly sweet smile stretched out on her face. "You're using again. Aren't you?"

You could hear a needle drop.

"What?" splutters Dawn after a beat, "what? How could you even accuse me of that...? I gave up that shit a long time ago."

"Yes, you did," says Faith, "and you were amazing. Now look at the state of you," she wrinkles her nose in disgust. "I saved your life, and then I trust you with my businesses, and this is how you repay me?"

Dawn's face crumples, and she takes a step forward, her sparse eyebrows sinking in the middle so that she is glaring hard at Faith. Out of the corner of my eye, I see Arlo's jaw drop. I can't help but find the same unease he must be feeling start to gnaw away like a rat in the pit of my stomach. People who stand up to Faith *never* end up better off. But Dawn is no longer just a person; rather, she is a broken shell of her former self, dead inside, rendered illogical by her addictions.

"Repay you?" squawks Dawn, hastily rubbing more sweat from her brow. "*Repay you?* You left us all. You just went. You abandoned us like we were nothing."

Faith laughs and folds her arms. She looks at Mischa, "you see why I am so particular about who I hire?"

Anger flashing across her face, Dawn stares at Hope. "Your mother was our leader. She made our family. Then she just left us. Not just that, but she left us with two criminal fucking businesses to run, as well as looking after a house, babies, and keeping the local feds happy...."

"How unreasonable of me to leave you with millions of pounds in cash, a mansion, and a newfound purpose for your lives which used to be worthless," Faith interrupts coldly. "I treated you *so* badly, didn't I, Dawn?"

Arlo stands up sheepishly and reaches out a hand as if to touch Faith, but he stops himself before his fingers brush her skin. He still fears her. You can see it as clear as day. "This is all a misunderstanding..." he offers weakly... uncertainly, to nobody in particular. "We were so happy to be coming back here. And we've loved every minute so far. The mission is still just as important to us now as it is today..." he blathers on like a pathetic idiot.

"Wait, what?" Hope snaps, cutting across his rambling, "criminal business? Sorry, what?" She turns to her mother, "who the hell are these people, Mum?"

But before Faith can reply and the altercation can unwind even further, Beau decides to sweep her big, meaty arm across the entire surface of the dining table. A god-awful shriek fills the air, making thought, or any other kind of sound, an impossible feat. Multiple dishes and glasses are sent flying in a mad frenzy across the room, liquids, and sauces congealing in the air and splattering like blood up the walls. She gets up from the table, dribble spilling from the corners of her mouth, and then throws back her head, releasing an even louder cry that makes the remaining glasses on the table tremble.

Instinctively, I push myself away from the table, my legs shaking as I hurry away from it. Daddy, Arlo, and Mischa follow suit, whilst Hope and Faith have the opposite reaction and both grip onto Beau's writhing arms.

"Pathetic, the lot of you!" snarls Faith over her daughter's shoulder, "you fuck up the businesses, you get back on drugs, I give you the chance to redeem your sorry selves, and you can't even do the one job you were given right!"

"MUMMY!" howls Beau.

Hope turns around then and shoots the rest of us a warning look, "get out, now!" she hisses.

We don't need to be told twice.

Hope

As soon as we wrestle Beau into bed and stick her with one of her sedatives, Mum shuts herself away in her bedroom. Part of me wants to follow her, to demand that she finally tells me what the fuck is going on… but it's overpowered by that other little niggling in the base of my spine… the one that screams that maybe I don't want to know the truth after all.

But could it really be that bad?

As it is, I know my older sister is a psycho murderer who eats strangers, and my mother uses the mutilated corpses for the good of science. Could it actually be any more fucked up than that?

Outside, I smoke a joint and swing absent-mindedly on the porch swing, my phone lying face up in my lap. Messages from my friends blink up at me, and my heart feels heavy as I long to spill out my soul to them. Imagine having normal worries that you could actually tell people about.

Just imagine.

"Hey…"

A voice suddenly tears me away from my thoughts, and I glance up to see D hovering a few metres away from me in the darkness.

I wonder how long he has been standing there.

"Mind if I join you?"

I shake my head, ignoring the disagreeable knot that tightens in my chest. "Sure."

I hear him pad softly across the wooden slats, then slump down beside me on the cushioned seat. I turn off my phone and take a breath, involuntarily inhaling the delicious scent of his aftershave, which gives me a tingly sensation inside. D is what my friends would call 'fit.' D is the type of boy my friends would be gushing over, the guy I should be aiming to lose my virginity to. If they saw a photo, no doubt they would be egging me on.

"Pretty heavy shit, eh?" he comments, sitting back on the chair.

I offer him the joint, out of politeness. "Yeah," I reply glumly because, to me, the evening's events haven't been heavy at all. I've become so normalised to spending nights cleaning the bloody remains of my mother's conquests; a stupid little argument over dinner is nothing. And in terms of Beau's outbursts, tonight *was* nothing.

"Thanks for standing up for my mum," D says next, taking the spliff from my hand. "I guess our mothers have a weird history we don't know about."

I shiver and instinctively clasp my hands to my upper arms. He wraps his arm tightly around my shoulders, pressing me close to his body. His scent overwhelms me, but it's no longer pleasant. It's sickly sweet, overpowering, like the scent of death and decaying flesh that I've grown to know so well.

"We've probably got a lot in common, you know," D says, exhaling a white cloud of smoke into the night's air. "We were both born into the family."

I frown and shrug him off, "sorry?"

"*The* family," he says conversationally, taking another drag of his joint. "Surely you must know? My mum says you don't, but I don't believe Faith would keep you in the dark."

"Keep me in the dark about what?" I ask. "What the fuck is everyone talking about?" I snap, getting increasingly agitated. "D, just tell me for fuck's sake. I don't know shit. All I know is my mum is rich and successful, and my sister is…." I stop myself before I can speak my mind. Beau *is* a fucking psycho. But as her sister, *I'm* the only one who is allowed to call her that.

D sucks on the joint again, then hands it back to me. "Do you not wonder about your father?"

"Sperm donor," I shrug impatiently. "Same for Beau."

At that, he raises his eyebrows. I can see he's taken aback.

"What? What is it?"

Awkwardly, he chews on his lower lip, avoiding my eye for the first time. "You really don't know, do you?"

Inside my chest, my heart is racing. Blood pounds in my ears, drilling deep inside the core of my skull. I can barely think. My next few words escape me in a half-dazed gasp.

"Know what?"

D's face twists, clearly bothered by conflicting thoughts. I grip onto his forearm and stare at him dead in the eye. "I want to know," I tell him firmly.

Silence trickles past for a few seconds before he swallows and finally looks back at me.

"Come with me."

I feel my heels dragging as I reluctantly follow D out of the house and down the street, the cool night air stinging my shoulder blades as I trail behind his hasty steps. He charges ahead, looking over his own shoulder a few times back at the house as if he is worried that we are being watched. We walk down to the end of the cul-de-sac, then he pulls me roughly into a darkened alley that I never even knew was there.

"What the fuck?" I snap, swatting him away.

"I don't want anyone to see us," D tells me, reaching into the pocket of his jeans and rummaging about until he pulls out a phone.

I fold my arms defensively and arch one eyebrow, "see us doing what, exactly?"

D doesn't reply, too busy swiping the touch screen of his device; his eyes narrowed in concentration, their irises lit up by the bright glow of the screen. "Here," he says finally, taking a deep breath and turning the phone around so that I can see it. He's showing me a picture of a huge house, even bigger than the one we live in. Outside are lots of shitty trucks and cars parked up on the gravel drive.

"What's that?" I ask, annoyed.

"That's where we came from," D says, sliding his finger along with the touch screen so that a new photo flashes up at me. This time it's a much smaller house, quaint and decrepit looking as if it is way out in the sticks. "And *this* is the farm."

"So?" I snap at him. "You're showing me these places. What does it even mean?"

A grim look passes over D's face. He takes the phone back and hesitates, staring at me intently as if considering what to do next.

"What?" I urge. "What is it that you're not saying?"

"Are you easily shocked?"

I frown, "sorry?"

"Are you easily freaked out?" D repeats himself, the serious expression on his face telling me that whatever *this* is, it is certainly *not* a joke.

I think about the countless times since I was just a little girl that I had to help my mum to clean up Beau's crimes. I remember how it felt to scrub blood from the floors, the iron stench of it suffocating in my throat. I think about the cold, lifeless stare of the corpses, their mangled, torn, and mutilated bodies surrounding them like a bloody halo.

"No," I say firmly.

D nods and swipes his thumb across the screen before turning it back towards me.

Immediately, I stumble backwards, and all of the air inside my lungs escapes me in one harsh movement. I clamp my hand over my lips and bite down hard on the inside of my cheek until I can taste blood on my tongue.

"What the fuck is that?" I muster, my eyes bulging as I find myself both horrified but unable to tear them away from the horrific sight glowering up at me from the phone screen.

The photo looks like something from a snuff film. It is crude... too crude to possibly be fake, like something from a horror movie. There's a man, laying on his side, apparently at the bottom of some kind of muddy pit. His eyes are wide open and grey, glassy and sharp, piercing me even through the lens of the camera.

Something tells me that the person in this photo is dead.

"That," says D with a sigh, "is your father."

"What?"

"Honest. They buried him alive."

He says it matter-of-factly as if providing me with a surprising but still somewhat acceptable piece of information. My head spins, and the contents of my stomach sours and stings.

"Fuck off," I shout, without another moment's thought. I turn on my heel and sprint back up the pavement, out of the alley, and back towards the house. My feet ache as they pound the concrete, but I don't stop until movement in the hedges surrounding our house stops me in my tracks. I pause, my chest burning as I frown and scan the darkness, my ears pricking. Maybe more stupidly than bravely, I force myself to go towards the sound of rustling and peer in through the stubby green clusters of leaves. My jaw drops as my eyes adjust and my brain registers exactly what I am seeing, lurking inside my mother's carefully pruned and shaped hedges.

It's Dawn. Her skinny frame slumped upright in a tiny, clear section concealed by the bush. I switch on the torch on my phone and hold it up, illuminating the space. Her face is ghostly white and shiny with sweat, her bulging eyeballs rolling into the back of her sockets, the whites of them yellow and bloodshot. In her lap, there is foil and a lighter.

Immediately, I know exactly what she has been doing. My jaw still hangs wide open as I back out back onto the concrete and bump straight into the same tall, lean figure behind me. Startled, I let out a cry of fright and spin around to see that D is standing behind me. Before I can run, he grabs me, clamping my sides with his big, strong hands. Just as I open my mouth to scream, he smacks one of his palms against my lips, muffling the sound.

"Just shut the fuck up," he hisses, "I'm on your side."

I writhe in his vice-life grip, but it's useless. I'm trapped there inside his arms. He waits until I appear to give up, too exhausted to continue fighting.

"Promise not to scream?" he whispers, eyes widening even in the gloom of the evening. Somehow, even when he has me like this, his moonlit face is undeniably handsome.

I grunt, thoroughly irritated that I have to succumb to him. He releases my lips, and I expel a long breath. My eyebrows furrow into a deep glare of annoyance so that he knows that I'm still pissed off.

"I know it's dark," says D. "Like... I know it's not normal."

"You're right," I snap, "it's sick to make that shit up."

D shrugs, "you wanted to know. So I told you. But you ran off before I could properly explain. It's a whole thing, Hope. The farm and the circus and just..." he trails off, "...I don't even know where to begin. To be honest, I don't feel comfortable talking about this so close to your house. Your mum is a dangerous woman."

Something inside my chest lurches. My instinct is to defend her. My mum isn't dangerous. My mum is the world's hero, champion of animals and the environment.

...but then there's that tiny flicker of doubt sizzling away underneath that illusion of certainty. It stems from the mystery that has always shrouded my mother like a cloud of thick smog and seems to grow with every passing day.

Maybe I should just ask her.

But then, a part of me is afraid to.

A part of me is still clinging tightly on to the doubt. My brain hurts from thinking it over too much, so I push it to the back of my head and then gesture towards the hedge behind me.

"What the fuck is up with your mum?" I ask, even though I already know perfectly well.

D rolls his eyes, "I can only apologise."

I know that I should be infuriated that my mother was right. Dawn, and probably the others too, are just a load of hippy druggy freeloaders. Lowlifes. Scum. In our house. Eating our food, smoking our weed, taking care of my sister.

But, as my shoulders slump and I turn and slope off back towards the house, I find that I am just too tired.

Pig

Fucked-upness aside, it's truly amazing to see Faith at work. Now I'm on the other side of it. I have more opportunities to really observe and analyse her process. Not that I could tell you what the process is. It's all just so sleek and smooth, like the mechanical cogs of a well-oiled machine, so seamless that even I find myself falling for her charms all over again.

I sit in the back of Faith's car and watch her chat with Mischa. Mischa was traumatised yesterday. Now she's sitting, excitedly musing as if catching up with an old friend in the passenger seat. Just like that, Faith has made her into another of her puppets, expertly twisting and turning her strings. Somehow gearing the young girl up, dazzling her into following the same sick, twisted path that she forced the rest of us down.

When we reach the lab again, though, the mood instantly changes. Mischa's face falls and darkens, and I sense her hesitation as the car crunches to a stop. Once the engine is turned off, Faith touches the girl's hand and gives her a small, patient smile. She says something softly, something comforting. It soothes Mischa. She is soon smiling again and willingly trotting along beside her new master back up to the lab.

Madness.

Once we're inside, Faith introduces me to an undersized individual who may well be the ugliest I have ever clapped eyes on. His face is almost shrivelled, whereas his eyes bulge out of twisted and wrinkled flesh. At first, I assume he must be one of her subjects, or maybe another of the mentally challenged cronies she has recruited, but this assumption is soon dashed when the guy opens his mouth and holds out his hand.

"Morning. I'm Xenon," he says in a distinctly snotty voice that makes me think of the stereotypical school geek. Of course, Faith would have needed some brains for the operation. "Today, you're going to be shadowing me. I'm going to be showing you the ropes."

I'm taken aback by this. I turn to look at Faith, who is watching me carefully.

"I'm not going back to the farm?" I ask, my stomach clenching with nerves like it does every time our eyes meet. Although it's been a while since I've been beaten, it's a painful memory that is still branded into the forefront of my brain. I can't forget it, ever. Talking equals pain. Faith, herself, equals suffering. "I'm not going to be helping out at the house with Beau?"

She licks her lips and tosses shiny black hair over her shoulder. "Don't bullshit me, Pig," she says, sparkling emerald eyes narrowing as she looks me up and down. "The farm is gone. So is the circus."

I don't say anything, remembering the stern warning I had received from Arlo and Dawn before we had arrived.

Faith smiles and shrugs, "it's not your fault, Pig," she says in what I think is supposed to be a reassuring tone. "I can't hold you responsible when it wasn't your job in the first place."

Still, I struggle to find words. Faith doesn't seem to mind as she puts an arm around Mischa's shoulder and smiles at the girl. "You and I are off to look at my latest project," she beams down at her proudly, "I think you're going to be just as excited as me. In fact, I *know* you will."

A few moments later, I am hurrying behind Xenon down a labyrinth of halls and passages. He doesn't speak to me until we reach a small room that is not dissimilar to another small room I used to know all too well. There's a glass section that looks out into a corridor and then a wall of screens showing security cameras. On a desk, there is a wide dashboard of switches, buttons, and flashing lights. All of a sudden, I'm back in the circus, controlling the sound and lights as hundreds of sick bastards file into their seats to watch unimaginable pain and suffering on the main stage.

The memory hits me so hard that it stings.

I find myself opening my mouth and speaking before I can think.

"Are you here by choice?" I ask bluntly.

Xenon does not appear fazed by the question. "Of course. Now, I've been told you have already visited the ward."

Ah, so he's in on the corruption. Of course.

I look through the glass and recognise the corridor as the one where someone had made an epic fuck-up and unlocked all the doors. The hospital ward of horrors. The cells of sadism.

"Faith has advised me that you will be in charge of the subjects. Their day-to-day care and... security."

My skin crawls. "What happened to the one before me?"

Xenon licks his lip impatiently and cocks his head, frowning at me as if I am an idiot.

"Dead?" I probe. I know I'm playing with fire, but this guy is so small I figure I could snap him like a twig if I really needed to.

"If you must know, many of the employees here have learning difficulties," Xenon tells me as if I should already know, "which is why we end up having so many... accidents."

Images of the mutilated subjects running and moaning down the hall fill my head; their eyes filled with impossible, heart-breaking fear.

"Faith trusts you," Xenon continues, nodding at me with approval, as this is some sort of achievement. "So this is your new position. You'll be paid well."

At that, I laugh. "She hasn't paid me in nearly twenty years," I tell him. "I hardly think she's about to start now."

Xenon doesn't say anything; he just walks across the room and gestures to the control panel. "It's a simple job, really. I do all the tests myself, and I have assistants to help me with the experiments. All you have to do is keep an eye on the ward, make sure we have no... incidents. Check in on each subject three times per day, give them their food and drink... raise the alarm if anyone has removed their IV or made a suicide attempt."

Bile crawls my throat, and I suddenly feel hot.

"Come," Xenon beckons and takes me to a small rectangular door at the other side of the room. I follow him down another passage that leads directly into the ward. Chemicals sting my nostrils. Against one of the walls is a metal trolley covered in trays. On each tray is a dog bowl filled with something green, mushy, and glistening. Beside the trays is a huge plastic bottle filled with cloudy-looking water.

"Each door has a peephole," Xenon explains, pushing the tray away from the wall and handing it over to me. "They also have a slot where you can put your hands in to hand over the food. There is also a tank outside each room where you can pour the water. The water goes into each room's plumbing system so they can use the toilet and have drinking water."

I daren't ask whether the two are separate systems. The trolley squeaks eerily as I follow Xenon, the wheels protesting under the weight of the trays and screeching on the rubber floor. "In room 1, we have a new subject," he tells me as we reach the first door. "She's very hysterical. I'd normally sedate her, but that would hinder the experiment." He rolls his eyes in annoyance as if the woman's trauma is a great inconvenience.

As much as I don't want to, I step forward and peer into the cloudy glass of the peephole. I look into the small, white box room. Inside, there's nothing but a seatless toilet, a tank of water with a spout (like the kind you find in a hamster cage), and a flat bed against the wall. I scan the area once, then twice, searching each crevice and corner for a sign of life.

"There's no one in here...." I say quietly. I'm just about to pull my head away when a face suddenly pops up in a flash of red and black in front of the peephole. I cry out, startled, and my heart thunders on the inside of my rib cage. "SHIT!" I yelp, stumbling backwards so that I bang into the trolley.

Xenon looks, then groans and shakes his head. "Jesus Christ. What a mess."

"What the hell has happened to her?" I stutter, my pulse aching through my entire body.

"Seems like she's pulled out her stitches," Xenon informs me grimly, "though it's not as bad as it looks. It was only an artificial wound. Probably not worth sewing it back up if she's just going to pick it."

I hear a faint moan coming from the room, although I can tell it's muffled, quietened by the heavy-duty partitions separating her from me. She's probably screaming. Crying out for help, just like I used to, all those years ago.

Crying for help that will never come.

Mischa

"I can't believe it!" I hear myself trilling faintly over the sound of my racing heart. I stop myself from clapping my hands together for fear of looking like an idiot in front of Faith. But I can't help it. I've been trusted with one of the world's greatest, most amazing secrets. It's taking everything in me not to jump up, embrace her, and smother her with kisses. "This is going to change the world, Faith...." I gasp, finally tearing my eyes away from the documents scattered on the low table in front of me.

We are sitting in a comfortable room, looking at charts and hospital admission papers. I have a vague understanding of it all, but Faith has explained the gist of it to me.

Faith has discovered a cure for cancer.

She smiles at me, "you see? It could have been anyone. But the thing I'm the proudest of is that I did it without hurting one single hair on one single animal."

A fleeting moment passes through my mind. Images of the horrific wounds on the human test subjects and the sheer terror and pain etched on their faces. But I shove the visual to the back of my mind. Criminals. Lowlifes.

"We're in the process of liaising with WHO," Faith says, "working out strategies for carrying out the distribution of the drug and such. But even when that's all done, I won't stop. If I can cure cancer, what else can I cure? HIV. Alzheimer's. Liver disease. Heart disease. Meningitis- the sky is the limit!"

I breathe out, my cheeks starting to ache from all the smiling.

Suddenly, Faith's face changes. She pushes her hair behind her ear and fixes me with an intense, serious stare, resting on her elbows on the surface of the table so that I am forced to look back at her.

"The reason why so many before me have failed is because of the rules. Society, the government... all these bullshit organisations and their regulations... it would be impossible for me to do all of these things if I played their little games and conformed to their rules." She pauses and licks her lips, never taking her eyes off of me. Her pupils penetrate me, burning into my skin like lasers. I feel the little hairs on the back of my neck stand up like she's sending bolts of electricity into my veins.

"You're special, Mischa," she says softly. "I have this... gift for sensing people out. For picking up on their energy. That's why my recruitment process is so... unusual. A person has to have the right... soul to work with me."

My cheeks flush pink, and I can't help but smile. Faith reaches out a hand and brushes her fingers on top of mine. Her touch sends waves radiating up my arms, causing my skin to break out in gooseflesh. I've never felt... *this* way for a woman before, but somehow I feel like I'm falling hard under a spell.

"You can trust me," I hear myself tell her, my voice dazed, monotonous as if I am in a trance.

Faith smiles, and it feels like a million vegan nut roast Christmases have come at once.

Jace and my old, shit life feel a hundred miles away.

Mischa

I wake up in the middle of the night drenched in a cold sweat.

Beneath me, the soft bedding that felt so luxurious when my head first hit the pillow is sticking to my skin, irritating my pores like tiny sucker pads. I blink up at the dark ceiling, my head awash with something invisible that I cannot quite put my finger on. I was, I'm certain, having some sort of nightmare, but I cannot remember what about. I push myself up in the bed so that I am sitting upright. All around me, the outlines of the bedroom furniture are eerily still in the gloom of the room.

I'm coming down from a high. At least that is what it feels like. Yesterday, after Faith had brought me back from the lab, the day had sped by in one blissful swirl. We ate, we laughed, we watched a dumb movie, and we talked about things... lots and lots of beautiful, colourful things, though I can't remember what. Now, that warm, fuzzy sensation in the pit of my stomach is gone, replaced instead by an awful hollow. I think of Jace and the one-sided text conversations ongoing between us. Yesterday, I barely spoke to him at all, too wrapped up in Faith. Now, I find myself pining desperately for him.

Clearing my throat, I swivel and get out of the bed. My mouth is painfully dry, so I pad across the room to the ensuite, switch on the lights and guzzle water from the sink. Droplets dripping messily from my chin, I come back into the main bedroom and scan the well-decorated area for my phone.

But it isn't there. And this realisation just makes me want it even more so that I can talk to Jace.

Wearing nothing but a skimpy vest top and my underwear, I exit the bedroom and rush down the staircase to the main living areas downstairs. I probably just let it on a table somewhere. But the moment I reach the landing and hastily push open the door to the living room, all thoughts of my phone are temporarily eradicated.

The light is on in the room, and the wide ceiling-to-floor bookcases against the far wall immediately draw my attention. They are no longer perfectly kempt, everything in its own specific place, but instead, books have been snatched from their shelves and haphazardly scattered on the floor. Some have been half-pulled out. Others have been opened and then discarded on wooden surfaces. In the corner of the room, kneeling down with her bony spine hunched over, Dawn does not even look up to acknowledge me. Her wrinkled hands scramble through the pages of a thick book, their movements frantic.

"Dawn?" I croak foggily, blinking in confusion as I walk towards her. At the sound of my voice, her head snaps around, and she shoots me an accusing stare. Wide-eyed and suspicious, she leaps up to her feet and reveals more of her painfully skinny frame. The sight of her is unsettling. She barely even looks human. More like a sick, scaly creature, starving and full of nothing but venom, scavenging for scraps of flesh to rip apart and gnaw on. I take a step backwards. My heartbeat quickens.

"I can't sleep," she says, moving forwards as if she is about to pounce on me. "I need my medicine. I need cash."

My mind floats back to the awkward dinner the day before yesterday, and it suddenly becomes crystal clear that Faith's suspicions were right. The woman in front of me could be the poster girl for a stereotypical drug addict. She couldn't look the part any more if she had a needle sticking out of her arm.

"I need money," Dawn repeats herself, quicker this time.

"I… I don't have any," I tell her truthfully. I don't know where any of my stuff is. Come to think of it; I can't remember having my purse anywhere near me since getting here. How did I not notice?

It's like the sick woman in front of me can somehow read my mind. Her pale lips turn upwards into a nasty smile, and her face half slumps as she fixes her cold, lifeless eyes on me.

"She's got you good," she tells me, knowingly.

"Sorry?"

"Faith," whispers Dawn, scuttling forwards surprisingly nimbly, never dropping her unsettling gaze. "She crawled under your skin."

I shake my head, "I've no idea what you mean."

But Dawn just laughs. "She's got a hold on you all right. Otherwise, you'd have run a mile. Or maybe you're just as fucked up as the rest of us."

My hand burns with the urge to reach out and smack her, but I resist the urge. "You're high."

"I wish I was," Dawn retorts. "There's only so much bloodshed one person can witness before being sober becomes torture."

"Just stop," I snap at her, "stop it. Look, you can't be rummaging through other people's shit, looking for money. It's stealing. Not to mention from your own friend."

Silence. I look down at my pale, bare feet on the ground and wonder what to do. Before I can open my mouth, Dawn speaks to me. When she talks, her voice has changed. She sounds sober as if she's been possessed, and her real self has fleetingly drifted to the surface.

"You know she's a murderer, right?"

I look up at Dawn, unsure how to respond.

"You think what you saw at the lab is fucked up?" she continues. "That's not all. She's done worse. She's a psychopath."

"Then why do you work for her? Why do you call yourself her family?" I counter back, arching an eyebrow. My resolution to Faith is fading by the moment, but I'm determined not to let Dawn know that.

Dawn scratches a sore on her chin. It rips open underneath her filthy fingernail and expels a thin trail of puss. "Why are you?"

"She's found a cure for cancer. It's a no-brainer," I reply firmly. "She's a good person, with a kind heart. I've admired her for years."

"Is that right? And what if I told you she ran an entire operation, slaughtering meat-eaters and turning them into dog food?" she wonders darkly, grey eyelids twitching.

"That's sick," I mutter, shaking my head in disgust. "I'm done." I turn on my heel to leave.

"What if I told you she charged people to come and watch other people get tortured? Or that she murdered her own parents? Or that she has a nasty habit of drugging people then kidnapping them, so they never see the light of day again?"

Without looking back, I break out into a run away from the horrible woman. I hear her laughing, cackling in that hoarse, cigarette-coated laugh. The soles of my feet slap hard against the floor in unison with every deafening beat of my heart. More sweat congeals on my hairline and dribbles down my back as I dash up the steps and run straight into a figure hidden in the shadows of the upstairs landing.

"Faith," I gasp, almost stumbling over backwards as her darkened expression comes into view. She's still beautiful, but her face has hardened. Her features appear sharper, colder somehow. I realise that I'm scared.

"Everything okay?" she asks me. I tell myself that I'm imagining it, but I could swear that she is being cold. She's annoyed. No wonder. It's the middle of the night, and I'm running around the house like a lunatic. My mind scrambles, a slippery rush of thoughts colliding so that my words come out in weird half slurs that mean nothing. I realise that I want her to make her smile again. I want to see her eyes light up and the corners of her smile turn upwards.

"Dawn," I blurt out, "she's… I think she's trying to steal money from you." The moment the words are out, it occurs to me that I have no reason to believe Faith would listen to me. By the sounds of it, she and Dawn go back a long way. She hardly knows me.

Faith sucks in air and purses her lips. After a few painful seconds, she nods in approval, although her words are laced in toxic venom. "Can't say I'm surprised. Fucking junkie."

A loud clatter startles me, and I see that Faith has thrown her phone across the landing, her pale face reddening and her brows knitting downwards in a fury. "You get back to bed, Mischa. I'm going to handle this right now." Before I can respond, she pushes gently past me and seems to glide eerily down the stairs, as if she's floating rather than walking. Something about the way she says it, more like an instruction than an offer or a suggestion, makes me plod immediately back to my bedroom. I close the door behind me, turn off the light and get back into the clammy bed sheets.

As I stare up at the ceiling, I realise.

I never got my phone.

Pig

Day three of being a lab warden draws to a close. My eyelids feel sore and heavy from exhaustion, physical and mental. On the hard, plastic seat, my backside aches, and my back protests every time I stand up. Worst of all, the feeling of being the absolute scum of the earth is still gnawing away at me, ripping my stomach apart from the inside.

I can't complain, not really. Not when I think back to where I came from. Waking up naked in a shit-infested van, crammed in beside hundreds of other sweating, wounded bodies, and then forced to eat and drink waste and sleep in an animal's cage outside. Having to mutilate and cut up dead human corpses as they hung from meat hooks, just to stay alive. Watching the love of my life die, then being made to sleep in a room plastered in images of her bludgeoned, lifeless face. Then spending every night watching countless innocents be tortured whilst a sea of people watched on and laughed. Having to scrape fragments of bone, innards, and other shreds of human waste off of a circus ring.

Compared to my past, having to look a person with severe chemical burns in the eye and tell them there's nothing I can do to help is pretty much a walk in the park.

I've grown to accept the sad, pitiful existence that has become of me.

"Pig." I almost feel my guts fall out of my body as the sudden voice alerts me to the presence hovering at the door. I jump and swivel in my chair. Faith stands in the doorway, watching me in a way that makes me feel like she's been there longer than I realise.

"Come, now."

Of course, I obey her. The years of trauma have conditioned me well, even though I could likely take her down if it were just the two of us. I've barely seen her at all the last few days, as she went away on business of some sort. In her absence, Arlo became a dick head again, strutting about as if he owned the place. In a way, I'm glad she's back. It gives me a kind of pleasure to see Arlo put in his place.

Faith takes me out of the building to the dark car park outside, where her car is waiting. She gestures for me to enter on the passenger side. Immediately, I'm suspicious.

I never get to sit up front.

"How do you like it?" she asks conversationally as I walk around the side of the vehicle, and she opens the driver's side door. "Xenon is nice, right?"

I nod, not wanting to lie but also not wanting to tell the truth in case I wind up being scalded with boiling hot water. This is a fond favourite response from Faith whenever anyone pisses her off.

Sighing, I get into the passenger seat and slam the door shut. I glance upwards at the lit-up interior of the car and catch a flash of movement in the rearview mirror.

"Shit," I blurt out involuntarily, as I turn and see that Dawn, Arlo, and Daddy are all squashed into the back seat, gags around their mouths, hands apparently bound behind them. "What the..."

Faith puts her key in the ignition of the car, and the engine rumbles to life. The light goes out, and we are plummeted into darkness apart from the illuminated countryside outside of the windscreen. She appears calm when I look at her face.

"We're all going on a little road trip," she explains absent-mindedly as she checks her mirrors and begins to reverse on the gravel.

"Where to?" I ask her, chewing anxiously on my lip. "Why are they...?" I trail off, not wanting to fuck her off with any questions.

The woman is unpredictable.

Before she answers, Faith drives onto the main road and begins speeding down it. I recognise the road signs for when we travelled up here.

"I want you to know, Pig," she suddenly says, "I don't hold you accountable. You were never a family member or recruit. It wasn't your job to continue my work. All you needed to do was survive, and by some miracle, you have."

"Lucky me," I mutter sarcastically underneath my breath, then instantly regret it.

Faith smirks. "I was wrong about you, Pig, all those years ago. And I regret how things turned out with Prue."

The sound of her name feels like a thick, clean dressing being ripped roughly and mercilessly off of a deep, raw, festering wound. So much so that I wince and feel like every molecule of my being is simultaneously souring and turning rotten. My teeth clench, and my fists tighten.

"I'm not always right," Faith continues. "But I'm making it right, now. You've shown nothing but loyalty to me over the years. More than these corrupt pack of scum bag junkies anyway." Her eyes flit to the mirror, and she shoots the coldest, sharpest glare at the three in the back. I'd always imagined it would feel good, having this kind of upper hand. The sort of advantage the three in the back had always had over me. But it feels less like a blessing and more like the death of me.

Realistically, I can tell we have been driving for hours, but the journey flashes past in a rapid blur. Faith talks at me. She asks me the odd question, but mostly she somehow seems to know everything. About the demise of the farm and the circus. About what became of the family. I don't lie to her. I want to live.

Fuck knows why.

As we pull into that familiar stretch of country road, my gut tightens, and bile crawls up into my throat.

"When did you start letting any old fucker into the family, Arlo?" Faith suddenly asks, putting her foot down on the gas. "Was it when you got too old to fight, or when the girls stopped fucking you?"

I can't look him in the eye.

The car stops abruptly, and Faith is pulling into a space at the side of the deserted road. She unclips her seatbelt, switches on the car light, and wrenches her body around to stare at him. She rips the gag from his bleeding mouth.

"When did you make it about the girls, Arlo?" she snaps. "It became all about the drugs, and the booze and the girls, didn't it?"

Eyes welling up with tears, he slowly shakes his head.

"DON'T FUCKING LIE TO ME!" Faith screams. "I trusted you, Arlo. But you never wanted to do my work. You just wanted the easy life. You pretended you understood, but you never fucking did, did you?"

Arlo sobs like a helpless child, "are you kidding me? I stood by you. I protected you and the businesses. I…"

"Shut the fuck up," interrupts Faith. She delves into her pocket and pulls out a piece of crumpled, lined paper. I recognise it as stationary from the address book in the reception area of the family house.

So she's been back.

Faith unfolds the paper, holds it up, and reads the hasty scrawl on its surface. "Who is Jem, Sonny, and Serenity?"

Instantly, Arlo's face drops. I hold my breath, nerves gripping hard on my windpipe so that I cannot let out a breath.

"Faith… please…"

"Who are they, Arlo?"

Fat tears roll down his cheeks, and he looks so incredibly pathetic. So weak. So old. I have never seen him in that way. I always expected it to be liberating, but instead, I find it a shock to the system. It's terrifying.

"They're my kids," Arlo croaks. "Please, Faith. Leave my children out of it."

Faith smiles, "you didn't mention you had children, Arlo. I'm surprised, as you know, that extending the family is another huge part of the mission."

His face crumples, and he shakes his head. He opens his lips, but words fail him. I almost feel sorry for him.

"Who's the mother?"

My heart sinks like a pebble in quicksand as I hear the question. She's got him good.

"Like what I was…." Arlo begins, his voice a squeak, "a sick person. I was just…."

"You picked up underage drug-addicted sex workers off the street and made them your sex slaves," says Faith. "Giving no thought to their age, no thought to their reformation, and more importantly, no thought to their relationship with animals or the part they would play in our work. Not only that, but you actually neglected the work I entrusted you with, so you could play out your sick drug and sex fantasies."

Cold, still silence.

Faith starts up the car, sighing disappointedly. Arlo whimpers and sobs, begging her underneath his breath, even though he knows deep down that it is far, far too late.

"What you did was wrong," Faith whispers, not taking her eyes off the road ahead. That's when I see the thick, black swirls of smoke rising up into the inky blue sky. "It needs to be fixed."

She slows down and swerves onto the drive that leads to the old family house. The huge mansion that Faith brought my work colleagues and me back to all those years ago. Where we were drugged, kidnapped, and our lives, essentially, were severed short. Even with the windows up, the intense stench of smoke infiltrates my lungs, near on suffocating me. I smack my hand to my lips as the horrific sight comes into view, lit up like a Christmas tree by the headlights of the car.

Immediately, Arlo lets out a loud scream of pain.

Faith pulls up in front of the blackened, smoking mansion. She is smiling widely from ear to ear.

"All fucking dead," she says distantly, eyes shining brightly at the scene before her. "Especially your kids, Arlo. I set them alight first."

"No…" his voice cracks.

Faith turns around again and taps on her phone screen before holding it up for all of us to see. She plays a dark, grainy video, the flash on her phone illuminating only three small figures bound and gagged, lying beside one another on a bed. I hear children crying and whimpering, the sound like acid in my eardrum, even through the tinny phone speaker.

"You fucking bitch…" sobs Arlo, "YOU FUCKING SICK BITCH."

I turn my head as I watch a match be ignited on the screen. I'm too afraid to cover my ears, so the horrific screeches of pain coming from Arlo's poor children in their last, awful moments burn onto every surface of my brain. I find my own eyes are welling up, and I'm struggling not to let out a low moan of despair. That last, minuscule shred of humanity left somewhere deep and buried inside me shrieks at me to do something. To destroy this monster. It wouldn't be difficult. I could snap her neck. I could let Arlo and Daddy free. She wouldn't stand a chance against the three of us.

But, here's the most twisted thing.

I do nothing.

Hope

How would I sleep without weed? I swear I've been addicted since birth, I'm sure Mother somehow laced her breast milk with it, and now it's my nightly ritual to smoke myself into oblivion.

I wake up and immediately see from my bedside clock that it is past 11 am. I lay there in bed for a while, clenching and unclenching my hand. I can't stop thinking about D and what he told me the other day. As much as my head screams that everything he said is some sick fallacy, I get this awful feeling creeping up my spine that he is telling the truth. I decide that enough is enough, and I need to speak to Mum. She can't be pissed off. How can she ever be pissed off with me? When she lets Beau murder men in our downstairs hallway on a regular basis?

So I slip downstairs, satin kimono wrapped around me. The house feels quieter than usual as I pad across the hall and down the staircase. I catch a glimpse of Beau through the slats in the stairs. She is sitting cross-legged on the floor, smashing plastic Peppa Pig figures repeatedly into one another, whilst singing her own rendition of Row, Row, Row Your Boat. I wonder what it would be like to be like Beau. Living in your own impenetrable world, unconcerned by the thoughts and actions of others. Satisfied only by ripping random humans to shreds, smearing shit over the bathroom walls, and watching children's cartoons. I quicken my pace, deciding I need a cup of coffee before I engage with my older sister.

In the kitchen, Mischa is sitting on one of the bar stools. She's staring distractedly into space, neglecting the single mug that sits on the breakfast bar in front of her, running her stubby fingers through the short spikes of her hair. Her pale, bare feet point downwards, her skinny legs hovering absent-mindedly above the tiles. I let out a sigh, unable to hide my irritation. All I want is to be alone.

"Morning," I greet her, forcing a smile and vaguely wiggling my fingers in her direction. "You alright?"

Her pointed features snap upwards, her intense eyes locking onto me as if she hadn't even realised I was there. "Morning..." she says finally, her words clearly tainted with unease. I had wondered how long it would be for Beau to do something completely disturbing and fucked up that would drive our new lodgers away.

"What's up?" I ask, although I secretly could not care less.

I sense Mischa open her mouth, then close it again. She's quivering. I clear my throat and pad across the kitchen to the coffee machine, not wanting to make the girl feel any more uncomfortable.

"You can tell me," I say casually, "if it's Beau. I know she's my sister, but... well, she's my sister. I know she does some pretty wild shit, and it's normally not pretty...."

"It's not Beau," whispers Mischa, in a strange, haunting voice that makes me stop what I'm doing and look up at her. Her eyes are wide and glassy as if she has seen a ghost. Fuck, judging by the number of bodies that have hit the floor in this place, it wouldn't be the most surprising of revelations.

"Dawn?" I sigh, switch on the machine, and listen to the familiar hum as it whirs into life. "I'm pretty sure my mum's going to kick her out," I assure her. As I say it, the grim picture of the unconscious middle-aged woman slumped in the bush with a needle protruding from her arm springs to mind.

Mischa doesn't say anything. I turn to face her and study her expression properly for a moment. Something about her sudden silence sends a prickle of unease down my spine, and my body involuntarily jerks.

"Mischa?" What's wrong?" I prompt, softening my voice as I move closer to her. I know I'm slightly younger than her, but I know I come across as older. You mature quickly when you're forced to clean up shredded corpses from a young age. "Come on, you can tell me. I know shit is pretty weird around here. Do you want to go home? I can call you a cab...."

"No." her voice is hard and sharp, like the jagged edge of a splintered glass, slashing through my own sentence. "No..." she repeats hoarsely. "I'm fine, honest." She gets up, leaving her mug behind, and stumbles slightly on the tiles. Her face is drenched in pure, unadulterated fear.

"What's happened, Mischa?" I try again then, swiftly navigating my way around the kitchen counters and blocking her path. The horror on her expression only grows by the minute, and it sets alarm bells off, ringing shrilly in my core. Before I can stop myself, I'm grabbing her by the arms, holding her tightly in my voice at length. I force her to look at me. "Mischa?! What is it?" It occurs to me, as I watch her breathing get quicker and deeper, that she's frightened of something more than some crack-head thief. And if it's not Beau, there's only one other person it could be.

"Is it my mum?" I half-whisper, moving my head closer to hers. "What is it? Do you know something?"

At that, I sense Mischa's lower lip wobble. Her expression cracks and her eyes swim light pink with tears. "I... I thought she was good..." she cries softly, so low that it is almost inaudible. "But then... Dawn... she told me about the farm... what they do at the lab...."

I swallow and loosen my grip on Mischa then. "You're going to believe *that* low life?" I question her, trying to sound intimidating. But still, that feeling in my gut pokes away at me, a far-off voice telling me that maybe I can't be so sure about my mother's real identity and her past.

"I didn't..." she replies after some time, so quietly that each word comes out muffled.

"What?"

Mischa doesn't wipe the black smudge pooling beneath her eye and appears not to blink or even breathe for the next slow-crawling few minutes. Just as I'm about to speak again and interrupt the deafening silence blearing on between us, she lets out a small, throaty sound, then speaks.

"I didn't believe a word of it. Not until I heard banging and shouts, and then I looked out my window and..." she cracks again, forehead creasing as if she is recalling a particularly painful childhood memory.

"What?" I snap, unable to hide my impatience.

"I saw your mum, shouting at Arlo, Dawn, and D. She was... threatening them with a knife. They were crying and begging so badly... I thought she was going to stab them, but I got scared and got back into bed..." she continues, the words falling out in fast, uncontrollable bouts. "I could never imagine her doing that… she's so chilled usually, and there was just something about the way she was talking, and the way she moved… like she'd done it a million times before…."

As I listen, my chest begins to pound, like a cannonball lunging in and out of my rib cage, tearing through the flesh, ripping skin.

I can't help but let the horrific scene play out in my head. *My* mum. A knife-wielding woman. A threat. Then I think about all the things she's been accused of. *My* mum. The murderer.

Hope

That little internal monologue in my head screams at me to kick Mischa out on her arse and cry profanities at her as she goes. But my instinct tells me she isn't safe out there, and, more worryingly than that, she might even be telling the truth. So, instead, I make her one of Mother's sedative-infused herbal teas and coax her back to bed. Then, I take Beau up to her playroom to stop her from causing unnecessary havoc, resume my place in the window seat and bury myself deep beneath the heap of troubled thoughts circulating my mind.

Outside, the sun is shining so brightly that it is almost patronizing, beaming down at me through the glass as if life is just fine and dandy. As much as I don't want to believe Mischa or D, it's beginning to feel a lot like the jagged pieces of a puzzle are slowly slotting together to form a sordid picture. From as far back as I can remember, death, blood, and guts were always just a normal part of my life. A part of my mum's life. Beau would frighten most fully grown men, but thanks to her, I have grown up fearless, unmoved by the dark. But that isn't normal. None of it is normal.

Beau grunts and I turn my head to look at her. She is snuffling like a pig, scribbling furiously with crayons on the hardwood floors. Better than more bloodstains, I guess. In a moment of madness, I get up from the window seat and pad over to her, squatting down beside my sister's huge body. She locks her eyes on mine and stops colouring for a moment.

"Beau," I whisper softly, reaching out a hand and placing my palm on her hairy forearm. She smiles, a thread of drool dripping from the corner of her lips as she does. "My big sister," I continue carefully. "What do you know about Mummy?"

She replies with some unintelligible but enthusiastic shrieks as if she is speaking in her own unique language. I study her eyes carefully, scanning for even the tiniest hint or trace of a memory. But there's nothing.

A car door slamming from behind me makes me jump. I get to my feet and hurry back over to the window, where I peer through the glass and see Mum's car on the gravel. Mum has just gotten out and is wiping her brow. She pauses, as if catching her breath, leans over the car with one of her hands on its roof.

I try to swallow, but my throat is as dry as sandpaper. An unexplainable dread ebbs away somewhere deep and entwined within my guts. She stays there for a few moments, her eyes trained down at the ground, her body still visibly heaving. There is no sign of the others.

I'm just about to get up off of the window seat to meet her when another noise roots me tightly to the spot. It is the rough, low growl of tyres turning on the quiet, desolate street beyond the leafy hedges, about to penetrate our bizarre, compact little bubble. Mother's head snaps upwards to at the sound, and we both watch as an unfamiliar, beaten-up old car pulls up to the house, far too close for comfort. I expect it to be one of her friends- maybe D or Arlo transporting a new car for her. Although what would my mum be doing with a piece of shit tin car like that?

My questions are answered when the car halts and the driver's door opens. A tall, thin young man only a bit older than me steps out. His arms are inked with tattoos, and he wears a worn-out old band shirt. I watch as he says something to my mum, his face pointed in a tight frown. I cock my head and hear myself mumble, "who are you?"

"MUMMY!" bellows Beau, right in my eardrum so that I startle and bite down hard into the back of my cheek.

"Fuck! Beau!" I hiss, cursing as I taste the rusty droplets of blood forming on the wet flesh in my mouth. "Jesus…" her huge figure squashes me into the side of the window seat so that I can only see a small slither of the outdoors, but I continue to watch the silent exchange.

Mum steps forward, slowly, as if performing some kind of dance. His face only continues to tighten, as if he does not like what he is hearing, but he remains fixed on that one spot. Then, eventually, he nods and is following my mother obediently towards the house.

"MUMMY!" shrieks Beau again, bounding out of the room like a crazed, gigantic puppy on steroids. I stare after her, one side of my mouth still aching as I force myself to my feet and pad slowly after her.

The rest of the house, I note as I wander down the upstairs hallway, is eerily still and quiet compared to how it has been for the last few days. Something makes me pause in the shadows on the top landing, and I cock my head to one side as I listen to my sister skip messily down the stairs. I hear the low rumble of voices and sense the skin of my palm grow clammy against the polished wood of the banister. I flinch as the front door slams shut and find myself swallowing back a foul taste that is congealing on my tongue.

More voices. I shift weight from one foot to the other as I hear my mother acknowledge Beau and usher her down the corridor as she often does on the rare occasion we have company. I lean over the bannister so that I can see a glimpse of my mother, her usually perfectly groomed hair slightly windswept and her pale cheeks redder than normal. I wait, expecting her to force Beau up the stairs. It would be the sensible thing to do.

I wait, and I wait.

Mum lowers her voice, and I watch as her lips move as she whispers something to Beau. I lean further across, straining my ears to hear the inaudible words rolling off of her tongue. I realise my heart is drumming loudly in my ear, and time briefly stands still.

A male voice slices through the tension like a meat cleaver through a joint of flesh, and no sooner than the sound reaches my ear, Beau's head snaps to the side. My stomach lurches as it suddenly hits me square in the face. My breath gets caught in my chest as it fights the horrific realisation now screaming at me inside my skull.

"No…" I croak, stumbling as I hurry forwards, my legs bendy and weak beneath my body.

But it's too late.

In many ways, it always has been.

"No…no…" I attempt to cry out, but my voice downs in an ear-splitting shriek. I fall hard on my knees at the top step but scramble to my feet and bolt down the staircase as quickly as I can.

When I reach the bottom, I see the young man, so oblivious and full of life just seconds ago. He is sprawled on the ground, crushed beneath the weight of my sister, bright red splatters of blood erupting from the side of his neck as she tears easily through the flesh. I clutch my lips and collapse on the bottom step. My pulse thunders inside my head as I watch her rip him apart like pulling meat from the bones of a roast turkey.

It's not the gore.

Not the blood and the violence that threatens to knock me off my feet. I'm used to blood and violence. I've seen more mutilated corpses than I've seen the sun, it feels like.

But it's the look on my mother's face that haunts me to the core, chilling every fragment of bone inside my body until I feel frozen inside.

She stands, petite arms folded across her chest, an expression of pure shock and horror saturated across her features. I realise, as she turns to look at me, her lips agape, that she is trying to deceive me.

The woman who raised me is a liar.

My life and my existence are a lie.

Unable to watch any longer, I force myself to my feet and half-stagger, half-storm out of the landing and down the hallway to the back of the house.

"Hope!" Mum calls after me. I ignore her as hot tears begin to well up and sting the corners of my eyes. But we both know that I cannot run or hide from her.

Nobody can.

"Hope!" she repeats, catching me with the firm grip of her hand as I enter the back room. I spin around to face her and am forced to stare into the dark emerald abyss of her eyes. I am temporarily transported back to my childhood, and all of my emotions turn on me at once.

"How could you?" I hear myself sob, my body falling limp in her arms.

She holds me up, not saying a word as she pulls me tightly against the soft warmth of her body. I let myself cry, tears leaking from my eyes, my chest heaving in huge, pathetic gulps.

"You know what your sister is like…" she says eventually, in a quiet, grim voice.

"You told her to do it," I whisper, whilst desperately wishing she will tell me that it is all just one huge, awful misunderstanding. "Dawn… Mischa…they are both saying the same thing…." I sniff, screwing up my face as I bravely pull away and stare my own mother down. "You're a bad person, Mum. You're killing people on purpose…."

She frowns.

"Sweetheart, this is all a misunderstanding. And I can understand why Dawn would lie, the pathetic junkie… but I've no idea why Mischa would say that against me…" she says, a genuine look of hurt washing over her face so that my heart sinks a little. "I guess she isn't who I thought she was."

"Why would she say those things?" I ask. I feel my eyes widen like saucers as they search desperately for a logical answer somewhere in my mother.

Mum sighs heavily and rubs her forehead. She lets go of me then and pads across the room, lowering herself down, so she is draped on one of the couches. I swallow nervously as I watch her massager her temples and stare distantly out of the large windows at the lawn beyond.

"It's time I come clean with you, Hope," she smiles sadly, still gazing somewhere into space. "I'd hoped to wait until you were a little older to speak with you about the business, but I can't have Mischa's misunderstanding trouble you."

"You mean you'll take me to the lab?"

Mother nods and sighs again. "This is why I am so picky about hiring people. It's too much for most to cope with. I've offered Mischa everything she could ever dream of, and she's stabbed me in the back with these cruel accusations… and to my own daughter as well…."

At that, I step forward, "it's not Mischa's fault," I tell her quickly. "I don't want her to get any shit for this. She was just afraid. I gave her some of your tea."

"Good girl, Hope," Mum smiles, "you're a special girl, you know. I'm so lucky, not just for you, but for your sister too."

My skin prickles uneasily. "So when will you take me to the lab?"

"First thing tomorrow," she assures me before delving into the pocket of her trousers and removing the slim leather of her wallet. She swiftly slips a brightly coloured card from one of its sections and hands it to me. "But for now, take the card and treat yourself and some girlfriends. Anything you want. You deserve a day to yourself."

Pig

I somehow fall asleep while on duty. I succumb to my heavy, sagging eyelids, apparently undeterred by my well-lit surroundings, and the next thing I know, I am waking up to an incessant tapping in my upper arm. I startle and almost fall out of my chair as my eyes flutter open and a zoomed-in view of Faith's face becomes apparent just inches from mine. Instinctively, all of my limbs tense up like a preyed-on animal preparing for impact. But when she withdraws and offers a small smile, I relax.

"Tired?" she asks, tight-lipped.

I mumble something incoherent and half-nod, half-shake my head. Truthfully, I'm not tired. I'm bored. And maybe it's the cocktail of drugs evading my system, but I'm sluggish and more drowsy than normal. Lazy, like an overfed cat sunbathing on a rooftop.

"I've got a job for you," Faith says, apparently uninterested in my response. "You're not busy here, are you?" She doesn't take her eyes off of me, her pupils like blades boring into my skin.

"Not at all," I reply.

I can't describe how I feel as I slope along behind Faith down the clinical-smelling corridors of the lab. I find that, more often than not these days, I can never really describe or even accurately identify my emotions. Over time, my entire inventory of feeling has festered and morphed into one hot, ugly mess, each emotion blending into another, crossing over in the worst ways possible. I mean, I can't remember the last time I felt happy. I feel okay when I'm buzzed. I've grown desensitised to the horror of mutilated bodies, human butchering, death, and suffering, so I no longer feel especially frightened or devastated. It's more just an annoyance when I'm sober, like waiting for a bus that's running hours late.

But what am I waiting for?

I hear croaks and shrieks echoing against the squeaky floors as I follow Faith. She doesn't acknowledge the sound, and I assume that Xenon is busy at work. I try to imagine being strapped down to a table, probed, prodded with rusty, illegitimate instruments, tortured by the beady-eyed man. I try to remember the gut-wrenching, mind-bending feeling of being trapped, encased in a fog of stagnant breath and relentless shackles, blood coursing furiously through your veins as each breath potentially becomes your last.

But I don't feel the way I did before. It's as though all the emotion is buried deep beneath thick layers of compacted soil, leaving me just a soulless shell. I don't feel sympathy. I don't even feel sadness or hurt as I traipse down the corridor of agony and suffering.

She leads me to yet another room I have been yet to visit. Not for the first time since arriving, it dawns on me how eerily similar the place is to the circus. Devised of a complicated maze of levels, passageways, and high-security doors, the very walls haunted by the panicked shrieks of its prisoners.

We step into a small space, where there is a large screen of glass from floor to ceiling just a few feet ahead. Through the transparent pane, there is a larger room, one of the rusted gurneys neatly positioned in the middle, a human-sized clump of fabric resting on top.

"A one-way window," I hear myself say out loud, recognising the screen as the same that I used to look out of on the circus control panel. Made of the same material that I used to watch people be humiliated and ripped to shreds through, in front of a live audience.

Faith nods and pauses in front of it. She clasps her hands behind her back and blinks intently as she appears to observe the image in front of her. "Mischa needs to prove herself," she says solemnly.

"Is that… her?" I ask, screwing up my eyes as if this will allow me to see past the sheet. "What do you…."

"Pig," Faith says sharply, turning on her heel to glare at me, "I have no time for questions. I need you in that room, and I need you to supervise Mischa whilst she… learns to be a butcher."

"A butcher?" I echo, temporarily misunderstanding.

"Yes," she snaps impatiently, "you know, how you used to be our guy at the slaughterhouse? Well, I'm telling you to revisit your roots. You need to guide her, and more importantly, make sure she doesn't run off."

"What? But…"

"Also, you will need to explain the task at hand to her," Faith continues, widening her eyes at me in expectation. "Look," she jabs a finger towards a darkened corner of the room, where I make out the faint outline of a solid container. "You have a tub to dispose of the parts. I have also left a pack of knives and scissors inside to help you. But remember, I want the girl to do most of the dirty work…" she runs her tongue along the inside of her mouth, "I'll be watching."

I blink, a thousand grisly images of brutally mutilated corpses strung up by their ankles, innards spilling out in a bloody waterfall, my hand warm on the knife as I rip and tear through flesh.

It's been a while.

"Who is that?" I ask, "on the gurney?"

Faith clicks her teeth again. "Someone that stood in my way," she replies simply as if this is all the explanation I should possibly need. She nods towards the glass, indicating the door. "The girl is in a waiting room through there."

I find my feet moving of their own accord, as if somehow Faith is inside my head, controlling me. It is, I think, strange to have one-way glass in this sort of facility. And a waiting room of sorts just beyond it. It strikes me then that Faith anticipated watching some sort of butchery when she first built the place. I briefly catch her eye as I press my palms against the door to the side and step into the room. Already, the unmistakable stench of pungent death surges into my nostrils and crawls down into my throat like a rabid spider, ready to lay eggs and multiply. Even when I can no longer see Faith, I feel her eyes upon me, watching my every move intently. Some small, inaudible voice shrieks at me from the back of my mind, willing me to grab one of the knives, dash back into the back room and slash the crazy bitch to death.

I could do it.

Nothing could stop me.

It would take her trained minions at least a few minutes to save her. That would be plenty of time to stab her straight in the guts. But then what? That'd be the end of me. Maybe I wouldn't mind that. Though I'd rather go softly, painlessly, not ripped mercilessly from existence by Faith's strange lab coats.

I open the door to the waiting room and find it is heavy on my wrist. The smell of disinfectant washes over me, drowning out the aroma of decomposition for just a fleeting moment. Sitting down on a wire bench against the far wall, I see Mischa, her skinny legs tucked beneath her chin, her face gaunt and pale. The narrow room is reminiscent of a bus shelter, plain and bare. Cold. I watch the young girl shiver, and her eyes widen as she scrambles to her feet which I notice are bare and dirty.

"Why have I been brought here?" she asks, her voice a croak. "What is going on?"

A sigh escapes me. I rub my temple and try to remember how this used to go. How I used to explain the very dark, morbid situation to any newcomers on the farm. How they had been drugged, ripped from life as they knew it, bundled naked and filthy into the back of a van, and transported to hell. How they now had one simple choice that could save or end their lives.

I chew my lip and glance back at the screen. Instead of seeing Faith staring back at us, I just see my own miserable reflection, standing there uselessly. I turn back to Mischa.

"You've just got to go with it, alright?" I tell her darkly, lowering my voice. "I know it sucks, but I'm guessing you already know by now that you're beyond having a choice."

Her chapped lips open, and she shakes her head slightly. I see tiny beads of sweat forming on her hairline. I take another step towards her so that I can hear the sound of her breaths quickening.

"You're going to have to cut up a body," I whisper, the words stale and vile on my tongue.

"What?" she echoes so loudly that it startles me.

Something inside me, a chain that has held strong for all these years, finally snaps. I grab her by the bony shoulder and yank her through the door back into the room with the gurney so that the door slams deafeningly behind us. She begins to weep, ugly-sounding sobs resounding from her spittle-moistened lips.

"Please..." she yelps, her entire skeleton shivering and trembling underneath my hand. I recoil, as if her pathetic, quivering flesh is burning lava, and swiftly pull the large barrel towards me.

"Take off the sheet," I tell her calmly.

"What? But…"

"TAKE OFF THE FUCKING SHEET!" I explode then, brandishing the weighty meat cleaver that has been left at the bottom of the large bin. I jab it into the side of her neck so that it nicks at the skin. It's just a tiny, artificial cut, but she lets out a wail of pain and staggers backwards. "DO IT NOW!"

"OKAY!" she screams back at me, every inch of her trembling as she reaches out her bony hands and touches the grim-looking sheet that is draped over whatever horror lies beneath.

Mischa

Bile crawls up inside my throat as the horrific odour only grows stronger and more intense with the movement of the sheet. Slowly, slowly, I pull it towards me, the glint of the butcher knife constantly flashing in the corner of my eye. A warning. A threat.

The inside of my cheek stings as the blades of my teeth chatter frantically against the flesh, the taste of my own rusted blood sickly as it simmers on my gums.

"HURRY THE FUCK UP!" Phoenix yells at me, although there's nothing left of the calm, quiet individual I have been sharing a roof with for the last week or so. His brown face is twisted, contorted so that it is ugly and thick with bitterness, radiating hatred from it like rays of unbearable sunlight. With my clammy fingers, I grip the sheet tighter and pull harder on the sheet so that finally, a pair of muddied and battered trainers are revealed.

My heart stops, then pulses so hard and so fast in my eardrum that I think I am about to die. Phoenix shouts something else at me, but the world is spinning, my vision swirling as if it's just some horrific nightmare swallowing me up like a tornado. Before I can stop him, he rips the sheet from my hands and tears it roughly upwards so that it falls to the floor in a grim heap.

I feel my jaw drop, and my heart snaps into two clean pieces.

A blurry video reel of those same red high-tops replay in my mind, the images scorching into the back of my skull. An unbearably hot day climbing a world-famous mountain, sweating hands clasped together, my head down, watching those shoes trekking along beside my own beat-up Vans. Looking up, a beautiful face lit up by the sun, the light shining on his glistening forehead…

"Jace," I hear myself squeak, stumbling forwards so that my arms fall onto his cold, dead chest. I force myself to look at his face. There's no smile on there now. He is wearing one of his favourite checked shirts, but it is hopelessly ripped, shredded at the collar. The side of his neck is non-existent, a wide, gaping wound that expels a foul-smelling discharge and soils what is left of his smooth olive skin. His face is smaller as if it has shrivelled up, and his wide-open eyes are sunken deep into their sockets, still glassy with terror as they stare up at the ceiling.

"Oh no," I cry, burying my face into his stiff, icy torso. "Oh no, no…no…." I keep on repeating that word, like an overtired toddler. As if saying it enough will make it all just some terrible, terrible dream that I will wake up from in a pool of cold sweat, Jace sitting up beside me in bed, drinking coffee and playing video games.

My hands travel around his body, searching… longing for even just a shred of warmth or life left in my dear best friend. But all they feel is death. Grisly, needless death.

"You need to cut him up."

At first, although I hear the words, I do not comprehend them. Rather they just rattle about in my ears like the tingling of bells. Then, I feel a hard nudge on my shoulder, and when I turn around, I see that Phoenix is staring at me, brow furrowed. In his hand, he offers me the butcher's knife. In the other hand, he holds an even larger, more menacing blade.

"The quicker you do it, the quicker we're out of here," he tells me stiffly.

In a moment of blind madness, I seize the butcher's knife and lunge at him, aiming directly for the centre of his face. In one swift movement, he catches my wrist and twists it so far and with so much pressure that it clicks. Involuntarily, I let out a screech of pain, and my hand releases the knife so that it clatters onto the ground, missing my barefoot by just inches. Phoenix rams me up against the wall so that the bones sticking out of my back feel like they are crushed. I sob even harder. I'm trapped.

"You've got to play the game, Mischa," he snarls, his face right up close to mine. "Just like the rest of us. If you don't want to play, you die. End of story."

His pupils are tiny and black, flitting about in their whites like the eyes of some insane, bloodthirsty creature on a violent rampage. I find myself searching them for some kind of humanity but find none.

"Please, don't make me do this," I whimper, "please... I love him. He's all I've got."

For a millisecond so brief that it could have been just a trick of the light, I think I see the man's face soften. But just as quickly as it appears on his expression, it has vanished once again, and I'm faced with nothing but a horrific monster from the bowels of hell.

"He is dead," Phoenix hisses. "And so will you be if you don't stop being a pain in the arse. You need to cooperate."

"Why?" I sob, "I don't understand. Is this because I said I was worried? Did... did Faith do this?"

Suddenly, there is a loud, painful whack in the corner of the room. In the doorway, Faith reveals herself, her expression cold and still. Unfeeling. Unmoved.

"Faith!" I shriek, "Faith help me! This is Jace. This is my boyfriend!" I begin to scream hysterically.

"I'm well aware of that, Mischa," she replies coolly. "This is a test. You said you wanted to be a part of my mission. Well, this is the price you pay. This is the cost of proving your faith and loyalty."

My jaw drops open. I stare from her back to Abdul, entire body pulsing with white-hot adrenaline. He opens his mouth as if to speak, then clamps it shut again. He grabs a clump of my hair and swings me back to the table. "You are going to pick up the knife, and you are going to cut the body into pieces. The pieces need to go into the barrel, ready for processing."

"No, please don't make me do this...." I beg, "please, I...."

I freeze, my mouth falling open as a scream gets stuck in my throat. I feel a sharp jab of pain in my hip and look down to realise that the harsh, jagged blade in his hand has sliced straight through a thin layer of my skin. The flap of flesh falls miserably to the ground and lands with a light slap on the ground beside the knife.

Faith licks her lips. I watch her from the corner of my eye. She looks satisfied. Content. Smug.

"Now," Phoenix growls in an aggressive reminder.

I scramble to pick up the knife and hold it unsteadily in my slippery palm, the pain searing through my entire torso. I briefly consider succumbing, just falling to the ground and letting him murder me right there on the spot. But then the sharp sting of the wound screams into my side, demanding that I obey.

Phoenix pushes me to the right so that we are standing by the side of poor Jace's lifeless head. "Start cutting the neck," he demands. "We have no use for that."

The world is fuzzy around me, just a blur of bright red and black as my tears form a screen over my retinas. I unsteadily hover the knife above Jace's partially severed neck, unable to avoid looking at the horrific gashes exposing ripped veins, tissue, and muscle. The dry blood stains chewed-up curls of skin on either side of the gaping wound, and my heart sinks even lower into the pit of my stomach.

"You ate him," I mutter weakly. "You… you fucking ate him."

"For fuck's sake," grumbles Phoenix, before slamming his hand down hard on mine, sending the knife hacking through what is left of Jace's neck muscles. Fresh blood splatters my face, but Phoenix lifts my hand and slams the knife down again into the same place.

And again. And again, until finally, the ear-shattering sound of the spinal cord being snapped cuts through the gruesome sounds of ligaments squelching as they are ripped through as easily as strips of paper.

Finally, Phoenix lets go of my hand. My knees instantly turn to jelly, and I collapse down onto the ground. Green bile pours from my mouth, saturating the blood-drenched skin on my legs. I retch and choke on my own heartbroken, disgusted sobs when suddenly I feel a sharp dig in my shoulder, which forces me to look up.

Jace's head dangles, slippery entrails crawling out of his severed neck like eels. His eyes stare at me, wide with shock, the stench now so unbearable that it makes me puke again. Phoenix holds the head and hits me hard in the side of the face with it.

It's heavy and wet.

It hurts.

"You'd better get fucking used to it."

Hope

I barely sleep the night before I visit the lab. Although I take up Mum's offer of a night out on her credit card, the whole thing just feels a bit stale. A bit half-arsed. A bit like a bright pink bow stuck on a giant shit, a sweetener to smooth over the fact that I was having serious concerns that I'd just caught my own mother feeding a real person to my sister.

On purpose.

But, at least my friends enjoy the evening. They always do. Maybe that's why I make friends so easily because people are attracted like a moth to a flame by money and notoriety. Surely that's how Mum gets everyone to bow down to her, somehow even without any true, meaningful connections.

Instead, I end up coming home early. Nobody is home, even though it's already almost nine o clock, so I just skulk up to my room, turn on Netflix and smoke blunt after blunt, shut up in the darkness like a recluse. The house remains quiet and still beyond my bedroom door, and I'm too stoned to force myself to care as to why.

Eventually, the seemingly endless cartoons dancing on my television screen blur, and I must fall asleep because when I wake up, the room is suddenly bathed in the light streaming from the outside.

The house is still silent.

I realise I'm still dressed in an old tracksuit, and the butt of my joint is still perched between my fingers, clinging on to dear life. I stub it out in the ashtray, then get to my feet, swallowing back the stale, dry taste in my mouth. I quickly shower and brush my teeth in the ensuite bathroom and then hastily scrape my wet hair back into a ponytail, shoving on a fresh pair of jeans and a plain t-shirt.

"Mum," I call out when I finally pad out of my bedroom towards the upstairs landing, "Mum, are you ready to go?" When she replies, I jump out of my skin. For some reason, I was expecting to be met with nothing but more thick silence.

"Yes, sweetheart, downstairs. Ready when you are!" she calls back, her voice bright and energetic.

Is that the voice of a cold-blooded killer?

Really?

I find my steps slow, and my feet become heavier as I go to her. When she comes into view, I see she is standing by the front door, rummaging through a bag. She looks fresher this morning than she did yesterday, less flustered and more like her usual self.

More like my mum.

The entire journey to the lab, I try my best to focus on the passing countryside beyond the passenger side window of Mum's car. I train my eyes on the turns in the road, the twists, and turns, the signs. But she has an uncanny ability to distract and keeps asking me questions that divert my attention.

As if she doesn't want me to know where we are going.

"So, how was it last night? Did you see I cleaned up Beau's mess all by myself? Did a pretty good job, I reckon," she chatters, pulling me from my own thoughts. At the mention of it, the image of the ripped open throat of the man flashes up in my mind. My stomach churns uncomfortably.

"How did you get him to the lab?" I ask, turning to her.

"Had some of the workers come by to help," she replies, never missing a beat. "They're used to transporting cadavers, donor bodies, and such."

"Donor makes it sound like he offered up himself," I comment.

Mum clears her throat, "he carried a donor card."

"What will you use his body for?"

"It will aid our cancer research."

"How?"

"Well, I can show you when we get there, can't I?"

I shut my mouth and turn my head back out of the window now, although it's no good. I like to think I know my neighbourhood pretty well, but I cannot recognise where we are.

Well played, Mum.

When we arrive and enter the infamous lab, I cannot help but feel completely underwhelmed at the sight of it. The place is not grand, or extravagant, or even particularly interesting to look at. Mum must read my mind as she leads me into the building because she chuckles at me.

"What were you expecting, a morgue?"

I feel my cheeks flush hot and red at the reference to my earlier accusations because that is exactly what part of me was thinking. I had envisioned this dark, creepy, old-fashioned asylum filled with mad scientists. In reality, it just looks like a hospital.

She shows me around some rooms, where complicated-looking procedures are being undertaken in test tubes and with microscopes. We're not allowed to talk. She shuffles through x-rays and pictures and diagrams in an office, bamboozling me with medical and scientific jargon that I zone out of quickly. All the while, I'm scanning every inch and cranny of the place, searching for even the slightest hint of something suspicious. But the more time I spend there, the more foolish and guilty I feel for ever doubting my mother. She explains the experiments through to me and tells me how they use the donated human matter to inject with cancerous cells and test formulas to combat them. She shows me an album and videos of all of the work the money she has raised for animal charities has done all over the world.

I even get to meet a few of her mysterious lab workers.

Mum leads me into a small break room, where there is a built-in kitchen, television, sofa, and dining table. On the couch, two workers in lab coats are nestled together, a young girl with Down's syndrome and an overweight, older man with greasy hair and a bulbous, red nose. They are cuddling, apparently engrossed in something on the television set, a bowl of popcorn balanced between them.

"Hi guys," Mum greets them cheerily, "how are you both today? This is my daughter, Hope."

The man opens his mouth to speak, but the words that come out are severely broken and incoherent. He offers a smile before shovelling popcorn ungracefully into his lopsided mouth.

"You remember back when Beau was younger, and I was just starting to get the business really going?" she asks me, turning away from the two. "I went through a stage of sending her to those groups."

"Vaguely," I nod grimly, remembering how eerie it would make me feel, dropping her off in the big house full of people who dribbled everywhere and smelled like urine whilst screaming and jerking in ways that did not seem human.

"Awful, wasn't it?" Mum agrees. "Well, I decided that I would give a home, a place of work, and a community for those people. One of the reasons why I do not have a recruitment process is because I like to give work to young people with special needs."

"To cure cancer?" I blurt out doubtfully but then immediately feel ashamed of myself for questioning it.

Mum laughs and shrugs it off, "of course not. No, they're more the muscle work... my assistants."

I look again at the two on the couch, and my eye is drawn to a flash of red at the bottom of the man's lab coat. I squint and frown, but before I can look further, Mum has my elbow and is whisking me across the room to a wide archway. Through it, there is a long room filled with neatly made single beds and more doors at the end, presumably leading to bathrooms.

It reminds me of an early 1900's orphanage.

But then I think about the conditions in the homes I had seen as a child and feel a glimmer of pride and admiration for my mum. She is giving them a purpose- a livelihood. An opportunity that they would never get elsewhere, where they'd been abandoned by others. And, from what I can gather, she is getting them to do amazing, revolutionary work that might end up changing the world for the better.

I start to realise how dumb I must be for ever doubting her, and for a couple of strangers, I barely know as well. Shame creeps into my bones as she continues to show me around the place. She continues to lull the burning itch of the suspicions that pained me so much before, explaining how the bodies are used for their cells to test out formulas.

Still, annoying as it is, my mind cannot help but continue to travel back to that flash of red on the lab coat.

Pig

I wait until I know for sure that Faith is busy entertaining her daughter. Showing her around the lab in its new, alien form. All night, she had me and Mischa cleaning the place up, tidying corners, concealing the ugliest parts of its sordid underbelly in preparation for the visit. The hours went by so quickly, as my sudden, random outburst of anger slowly but surely dissipated until there was nothing left but shame and self-hatred. I'd let myself turn into the monster. I was succumbing, finally, to the brainwashing. Starting to think like a true family member.

Mischa sits, curled up in one of the back waiting rooms on a fabric armchair, her skin waxy and white, eyes sunken and hollow like a zombie's. She doesn't look up as I enter the room, her expression vacant as I approach her, then slowly sink down to my knees so that I am no longer towering above her.

"Mischa. I'm sorry," I whisper. I try to sound strong, self-assured, but my voice breaks, and I realise that, for the first time in a long time, tears are welling up in my eyes. "I'm not one of them. She took me. And I've just been here for so long. There's nothing left of who I used to be."

She looks up at me then, and I see her throat bob as she swallows. "How long?" she questions me.

"About twenty years," I reply.

Her face crumples, and she shakes her head slightly, "have you never tried to escape?"

I sigh and think carefully about how to respond. I come up with nothing that makes me sound less pathetic or any less demented and twisted than the rest of them. So I go with the truth.

"A long time ago, my…someone I loved, broke me out of the farm. It was a terrible place, and so difficult to get out, but we managed it…" a small smile creeps up at the corner of my lips as I remember the night, lying with Prue beneath a tree.

Part of me genuinely believed then that we had done it. We'd broken free.

"...but they found us." I sigh. "They killed her. Then they cut her up, mutilated her almost beyond recognition, and forced me to sleep in a room covered in the photos of her corpse."

"So I suppose it felt really good to put someone else through that same pain of seeing the person they love most in the world be cut up," she snaps coldly. "I don't feel sorry for you, Phoenix."

"It's Pig, actually."

Mischa whines and runs her hands through her stubbly hair. She chews down on her lip and glances around at our surroundings. "So is that why Faith gives you so much freedom? Because she knows you're too afraid to try to leave again?"

I stare at her. The pain and the fear etched into her features is so fresh and so raw. She's traumatised but not beyond help. She's still a living, breathing human with warm blood and a heart that beats, and a conscience and a mind that can love and hate. My fists clench and unclench, and I realise they have grown clammy with sweat.

"You said you're not one of them," she adds suddenly. She softens. "So why don't you prove it? We can get out of here..." she whispers.

"It's not that simple."

"Isn't it? Faith is dangerous. And you have the power to get us away from here. You have the power to..." she chokes over her words, "... you could help me to get justice for Jace."

My wrist aches with the weight of his severed head, and I can feel the grease-layered hair that I held the dripping article up with. I hit her with her boyfriend's decapitated head.

I did that. As I often do, I imagine Prue sitting somewhere up in the sky, lounging on a cloud, staring down at me in despair. In disgust.

"Pig..." Mischa breathes, suddenly clutching my skin with a sense of urgency. "Pig, you can save us."

The skin on my back tingles and prickles up and down my spine, and I find myself shuddering. Her eyes are widening, searching as she blinks frantically at me, as though at any moment I might disappear, plummeting her back into a hopeless place.

It's then that the alarm goes off.

Hope

Mum and I are just approaching a heavy set of double doors made of iron when the deafening shriek of a siren interrupts the string of scientific jargon pouring effortlessly, smoothly from her lips. Her face drops, a fleeting, brief expression of alarm crossing her face.

It's gone just as quickly as it appears.

"Is it a fire alarm?" I ask her over the din, clamping my palms over my ears.

She opens her mouth like she is about to reply to me but then shuts it again as if she thinks better of it. Instead, she grabs my forearm and pulls me urgently to the door, tapping in a code that releases the opening. I am tugged into another metallic room that smells of disinfectant and is lined with bookshelves and a few computers on desks.

"Wait here," she instructs me grimly, "I won't be long."

And just like that, she's gone again, leaving me by myself in this strange, laboratory slash library. I swallow and release my ears, although the sound is beginning to make my head pound. I glance around at my surroundings and replay my mother's orders.

I decide against them.

I march out of the room to find that the corridor outside is deserted, but there's only one direction that Mum could have gone, and I am hoping that the incessant bleating of the alarm will drown out the sound of my footsteps. I hurry along, my curiosity forcing my feet to move quicker than usual. If it was some sort of fire, surely Mum would be getting me out of the building, not leaving me in some tin can ICT suite.

When I start approaching doors (and there are lots, far too many to show me them all, according to my mother), I push each one to see if they'll budge. As I suspected, the little control panels next to each one must be password protected. I cannot help but wonder why. Is everything here really so classified when the only people who ever come here are the employees?

Still, I keep going, regularly trying the doors dotted on either wall as if there might be a rogue one that is on a latch. But I have no luck, and soon I find myself at a crossroads in the labyrinth of grey passages. There are no signposts or printed letters on the walls giving any sort of direction. In fact, it's baffling to me how anyone could ever find their way around. It's like one big, never-ending maze that I have been sucked deep into the belly of.

A tug from behind me on my elbow startles me, and I let out an involuntary yelp which is immediately silenced by the wails of the alarm. Powerless, I flail backwards, my heart pounding so hard that I think it might explode inside my chest at any moment.

"Sssh!" a barely audible voice hisses in my ear, hot splatters of saliva landing inside the drum.

I spin around to see that Phoenix is standing behind me, pupils wide and frantic with urgency. A concealed door that is camouflaged by the same panels on the walls is open, revealing itself. My breath gets caught in my throat when I see Mischa standing there, her face ghastly with fear.

Phoenix mouths something at me that I don't understand, then grabs my wrist and pulls me towards the dark opening. For some reason, I let him take me.

Inside the wall, the air is hot and dusty and smells like wood chips. It reminds me of the backstage of a performing arts school I used to attend as a little girl. Once the door is closed, the ring of the siren is muffled slightly and continues to quiet as Mischa hurriedly leads me away from it.

"What the hell is going on?" I finally muster once the furious rings are distant enough. "What is that siren? Where are we?"

Wordlessly, as if I have not spoken at all, Phoenix stops and feels about on a random spot on the wall to his left. I pause briefly, then glance back at Mischa. I can see her eyes are red, puffy, and exhausted. She's been crying. More than that, she looks as though the very essence of her soul had been drained from her body, like the blood from a slaughtered pig. I step forwards and wrap my arms around her, but her skinny frame stays stiff and rigid in my embrace.

"Mischa? What has happened?" I ask again, this time louder and firmer. "You look awful. What are you doing here?"

The young woman sniffles. Before she can answer my question, a light suddenly floods the gloomy, narrow passage, and a big rectangular panel running along one side glows brightly. Quickly, the lights fade into an image, and I realise that I am staring out of a window, straight out into a part of the corridor where I had just come.

"What the hell is this?" I gasp, pressing a palm up to the glass. I turn to Phoenix, "what is going on?"

He arches an eyebrow and stares at me intently, deep, piercing brown eyes boring deeply into my core. "You really don't know?" he questions me after some time. "This isn't all just some act you put on to help lure people in?"

I feel my face crumple with confusion. "What the fuck is going on?" I ask again. "I haven't got a clue. Please enlighten me. It's the only reason I ever wanted to come to this fucking place."

"Your mother, it's all true," blurts out Mischa, her cold, bony fingers grabbing at my shoulder. "She's a fucking nut job. She just…" she trails off then, and I sense Phoenix shooting her a glare of warning. My skin prickles. I realise that they are both waiting, watching to see how I react.

I sigh. "I've heard so many different versions of events over the last few days," I tell Phoenix. "And I don't know what to believe. Maybe it would help if you just tell me everything."

"We'd be here for ages…."

"Hope," Mischa says, grabbing me again, her nails digging into the flesh around my elbow. "Let me show you."

A bit like on one of those claustrophobic reality TV shows, I discover that we are in a tunnel in the wall which has built-in, touch-activated one-way glass. The lab is literally designed so that you can hide in the walls yet still see everything that is happening without anyone realising it. As I trail along behind Mischa, my brain hums as it tries to decipher why and how my mother would want to build such a structure. For what purpose?

Soon, it all becomes horrifically clear.

When we reach another doorway in the tunnel, Mischa abruptly stops and turns around. "Brace yourself," she tells me grimly. "It's fucking disgusting."

"What is?"

Without a word, she places her palms on the door. I turn back to Phoenix, a vile taste congealing in the back of my throat. He will not meet my eye. I don't find myself afraid of him or Mischa. Or even of whatever it is beyond the next door. It's all the questions swirling around like an insatiable vortex in my brain that irks me, causing my brain to hurt and goose flesh to break out all over my skin. I have so many things I want to ask, but something makes me turn and follow Mischa over the small threshold into the next area of the narrow wall tunnel.

Slowly, as if it is leaking in through the glass rather than slamming me straight in the nose, the stench of burning flesh stings my nostrils. Instinctively, I put my hand up to my lips and swallow back hot stomach acid, blinking as I turn my head and squint through the glass.

It feels as though we are in a zoo. Not that I would know what it is like to visit a zoo, considering the intensity with which my mum shuns and resents them. She always said how animals have the right to roam free, maybe even more than humans. Superior and entitled by innocence. Now, I find it ironic that the woman who protested against a big cat sanctuary has designed a building filled with small glass boxes.

Once I've adjusted slightly to the foul stink that clings to the air, I blink and train my eyes hard on what lies beyond the glass, inside the monkey's cage. At first, I assume it's just another of the employees that Mum has taken under her wing from the care home because the room is like a small prison cell, with nothing but an unforgiving-looking bed. But the longer the look, the more I see. On the bed is what appears to be a small bundle of rags, lying curled up into a ball on the bed. I startle when it moves suddenly, an angry red scalp suddenly coming into view.

"What the fuck?" I gasp, stepping backwards, my back slamming into the wall behind me, sending a sharp pain into my shoulder blades.

At the sound of my voice, the shrivelled, oversized turkey head spins around. "What the fuck?" I shriek again, my knees knocking, desperate to run but with my feet frozen to the ground.

"Hello?" the deformed creature on the bed calls out. It springs up from the bed, its movements jerky and sharp, overly so as if it's on some kind of drug. "Is someone there?" it wails, dragging itself forward. As it comes closer, I see that it does not blink. Red, bulbous eyeballs stare at me, full of terror, and I soon realise that the eyelids are gone. The rest of the flesh is raw, wrinkled, and thinning, stained with pussing blisters. The smell somehow seems to worsen. I turn to run, but Phoenix grabs tightly onto my arm.

"Get the fuck off me," I snap, trying to pull away, but he does not budge, forcing me to remain in place as the vile prisoner staggers closer to me.

"Is anyone there?"

"He can't see us...." Mischa whispers, her features saturated in shock. "This is... oh god... this is what she meant when she said about observing subjects...."

Phoenix smirks grimly. "This is nothing," is all he says, those three words hovering in the air like a bad, haunting stench.

"My mum did this?" I ask.

"Well, it's her lab," Phoenix replies, "so what do you think?" he turns to me then, and I find myself locking eyes with him just to get the image of the caged burn victim out of my sight. For the first time since we met, I see a sliver of emotion glinting in his deep, intense brown eyes. I see the reflection of a memory; a peek through a window into a nightmarish past. "You were suspicious of your mother this whole time," he says, "and there's a reason why you weren't brought up like Daddy. Brought up to believe that this is all normal."

"Daddy? What..." I trail off, and it dawns on me.

D.

"Two babies were born. Faith was so pleased with herself," says Phoenix bitterly. "Two babies born from the cult, sorry, *the family*. There was Daddy, and then there was Beau. Of course, Daddy wasn't kicked the shit out of and drugged in the womb."

My face crumples. "What?" Immediately, a horrible image of my mum, heavily pregnant and abused, floods my mind. Just as quickly, the picture is torn apart by reality. My mother? Kicked the shit out of? I'd more likely believe that Beau won a beauty pageant.

Phoenix seems to read my mind. "I'm not talking about your mum, Hope. Faith isn't Beau's biological mother. Her biological mother and father were my work colleagues. We were on some bullshit work retreat that I only ever went on to try and get to know... someone."

I'm not sure if it's the gloom and the light from the room, but I swear I see a glisten of a tear swimming in his eyes.

"What the hell?" is all I can muster. "What, and you fell in with my mum's cult? Is that what you're saying?"

Phoenix chuckles and shakes his head, "oh, oh how I fucking wish it had been as pleasant as her grooming us and persuading us to join of our own free will. She fucking drugged us. Next thing I know, I'm waking up naked, packed in the back of a shit-smeared van with hundreds of others. A third of us were trained to be butchers, forced to cut up another third and mince them into animal meat. This is what happened to the others," he nods at the glass, where the mutilated victim continues to whine and smack its head hard against the floor. "Faith had a mini-lab back then. She'd experiment on some of her prisoners. I think that must have been the worst fate of all."

I breathe in and out, the world spinning around me as I try and repeatedly fail to comprehend what he is telling me. For a moment, I debate coming to my mother's defence, accusing him of lying and flying off the handle. But suddenly, the final piece of the puzzle clicks into place, and everything all makes sense.

Beau isn't violent by nature. The only ones she has ever killed are the ones Mum brought into her house. Like dangling a baby mouse over a snake tank. And Mum uses the bodies for the lab. As if it was a method of disposing of the evidence. As if she was protecting Beau.

"Why?" I hear myself whisper.

Mischa touches my hand, pressing the pads of her fingers gently to my palm. I flinch.

"I don't think that matters at the moment," she tells me softly, "what matters now is what we are going to do."

I laugh, close to hysteria. I turn to her. She looks so small and weak.

"And what makes you think I'm not in on it all?" I demand, forcing myself to sound braver than I feel. "You're both pretty fucking confident, aren't you? This is my mum you're talking about *and* my sister."

Phoenix touches my shoulder, forcing me to spin around. I shrug him off, my brow furrowing, furious at him for dashing my vision of my mother. Almost as much as I am furious at myself for never seeing it before.

"There's a reason why your mother uses Beau and not you," he tells me calmly, apparently undeterred by the hostility of my reaction. "There's a reason why she didn't raise you like Daddy or even Beau. And that's because you're smart. Just as smart as your mother," he pauses briefly, his face darkening. "It fucking terrifies her."

"Sorry?"

He moves his face closer to mine. "You've got the potential to be Faith's match, whereas no one else has ever come close. There's only one difference, the childhood trauma."

At that, I laugh. "I'm sorry, I don't think you realise what walking into a blood bath and seeing a ripped-up human corpse in the kitchen at four years old is like."

"That's exactly my point," Phoenix says. "You grew up with all of this fucked up shit, and yet somehow you don't have this innate desire to hurt and kill, to torture and destroy. Not like Beau and Daddy, who are victims of their environment. You're made of tougher shit."

I close my eyes, unable to believe the whirlwind that has become of my life over the last week. I'm trapped in the middle, and everything is spinning so fast all around me that I can't even begin to think about what is wrong and right. About what my next move should be. It's scary and confusing, but there's one thing the most terrifying of all.

Am I going to have to turn on my own mother and sister?

Mischa

A few moments of stunned silence pass before Phoenix indicates for me to continue leading down the narrow passage. We walk, from then on, in silence. We move away from the room with the poor man with chemical burns and pass about five or six others. They haven't all been burned.

In the next room, a limbless body is strapped to a stationary gurney. The face is trapped in a brace, staring up at the ceiling, the face raw, red, and cracked with tears. Like a starfish, the bloody stumps where the arms and legs should be quiver and jerk all around. The woman whimpers and cries, begging to be killed.

Another room has a young man sitting upright in a chair, a thick bandage wrapped around his head. His eyes are open, but the pupils lol in opposite directions, and a thick web of drool drips from his cracked lips.

Adrenaline courses through my body, and it is the only way I don't keel over now and pray to God someone kills me and ends it all right now. How the fuck do I live after this? How the fuck am I living now? My head pounds, reminding me of the way Jace's dead, rotting skull was aimed at me and how the last time I saw him, he was encouraging me to come to this God-awful place.

"SHIT!" I yelp, my entire body tensing as something slams hard against the one-way glass to my right. I turn to see what appears to be some kind of hoof smashing into the pane, splatters of blood erupting all around it in a grotesque, sticky halo. Horrified, I press my back up against the other side of the passage. The hoof is withdrawn, and I see the manic, shaking figure of a skinny, naked man rushing back and forth. At first, I think he's holding a decapitated cow leg, but as the steam on the glass clears, I realise that the leg is protruding from his abdomen. Around it, green and brown lacerations of infection are like spider legs coming from the wound, shocking in colour against the creamy waxiness of his skin.

"GET ME OUT OF HERE!" he bawls, ramming himself forward again. The glass shrieks and threatens to crack but remains unscathed.

Even five minutes later, when we finally reach the end of the passage in the wall, the sound of his screams echo like smashing glasses in my eardrums, the image of the severed cow leg ingrained deeply in my skull.

Suddenly, I'm hot, and I'm finding it hard to breathe, stifled by the claustrophobic atmosphere. Hurriedly, I reach out for the door handle, but Phoenix yells at me to stop before I can. I turn back to see him standing there, that hardened, serious expression on his face. I see Hope, just a teenage girl, her face wet and smeared with tears, her lip wobbling as she somehow tries to hold her shit together.

"We can't just go out there like this," Phoenix hisses sharply, gesturing towards Hope and me. "If we're serious about finally putting an end to this chaos, we have to be smart about it."

"It's three against one," I whisper, "we'll just lock her up. Call the police."

Phoenix tuts and shakes his head as if I'm incredibly stupid and naïve. I suppose I am. But before he can speak, Hope chimes in. "My mum is pretty much untouchable," she says through her tears, "I've seen her get away with so much shit. It's all the money. And it wouldn't be three against one anyway because she's hired hundreds of Beau's to fight for her. We wouldn't stand a chance."

My heart sinks, my skin prickling. "You don't know that...."

Hope laughs humourlessly and rubs her temples, "my sister can rip a fully grown man in seconds..." she mumbles, "and I know the others aren't as big as her, but there's a lot of them. And they're all just as mentally vulnerable as my sister, no doubt they'd jump off a fucking cliff if my mum asked them to."

Silence falls over us as the grim reality settles in.

"We've got to be clever," says Hope, turning to Phoenix. "I agree. We have to get out of here. You pretend you found me, got me back," she nods at me, swallowing nervously, "Mischa helped too. She could do with getting in my mum's good books."

Phoenix nods slowly, "ok... but then what?"

"I tell my mum I want a night in," Hope replies, biting down on her lower lip as the gears in her mind whir, and her pretty eyes crinkle with concentration. "I can distract her. Then you release everyone here, get everyone to safety… when my mum realises, she'll get my sisters and me on a plane to somewhere else."

"But what about you?" I ask her.

She gives me a small, bitter smile. "I don't want her to do this anymore, and I don't know if I'll ever look at her the same, but I'll be damned if I turn her in. She's my mum."

I feel a dull pang in my own chest as I think of my own family and parents. What I'd give to be somewhere warm and safe right now. Phoenix appears to feel it to, because I hear him sigh heavily, shaking his head, a melancholy twist in his lips.

"It's just so ironic," he mutters. "You know, over the years, I heard snippets of your mum's story. She had a rough childhood. A drug-addicted mother and her abusive boyfriend. I don't know the exact details, but I know that whatever it is fucked her up. And now, here we are."

"And how is that ironic?" Hope asks, "because I'm loyal to her?"

"No," Phoenix shakes his head, "because her mother fucked her up. Now, *she's* fucking *you* up."

Pig

For almost twenty years, I've wondered when it will all end. It crossed my mind every day, although granted with less frequency and urgency as time went on. Definitely much less when Faith left her sick, twisted legacy in the hands of a bunch of degenerate junkies, and I learned to silence the voices with whatever drug I could get my hands on. But I've not felt this sober in a long time, and my future feels crisp and clear-cut in my mind for the first time in years. Just like in the early days, when a stupid part of me thought that there would indeed be an end, I constantly think about Faith's demise. I picture it in my head, watch the thick scarlet river leak from her perfect, smooth neck. If I close my eyes, I can hear the rasping echo of her shrieks spiking like razors in my eardrums as the life drains quickly from her veins. On my fingertips, I can feel her flesh turn cold and limp, and on my tongue, I taste rusty blood spatter as I lick it slowly from my lips. And, that old, familiar stench of rotting meat has never smelled sweeter as it congeals in my nostrils.

I lay in my bed, a narrow but fairly comfortable slab in the corner of my bedroom, on one of the top floors of the lab. Faith had promised me a bed in the house, but this suits me much better. It means I get to be here all the time. And better yet, it means that Faith Farmer trusts me, which in turn means that she is finally losing her touch. No longer as sharp or sly anymore. She fell for my act.

When I can take no more of blinking up at the ceiling, I get up. I'm still wearing my shoes, fully dressed. Out the window, I can see the sky is a dark, inky blue. Hope was certain she could keep Faith distracted. Obviously, there's the possibility that it's all a set-up, but at this point, I have nothing to lose. I can at least cause as much damage as possible before I finally get taken out.

Before I leave the small, slightly stuffy room, I crouch down beside my bed and rummage around beneath it for the small, plastic container I had managed to smuggle away from the lab earlier on. Squatting back on my heels, I peel off the lid and retrieve a small bottle of clear liquid, raising it up to my eyes for further inspection. Before I can think too much, I twist off the screw-top and take a swig of the foul-tasting chemical. The moment the poison hits the back of my throat, it stings, and my entire face screams in pain as the liquid sizzles against my damp flesh. I force it down, only barely appreciating the instant warmth it sends shooting down into my stomach. I hadn't planned on drinking more than one mouthful, but I find myself taking three in total, which is a risky business. One swig is probably enough to get you buzzed, but any more than that and fatal ethanol poisoning becomes a very real possibility. I learned that in my old life, strangely enough. It's odd what you remember.

Coughing back the foul aftertaste, I shove the almost empty bottle back beneath my bed, get up and smooth down my clothes. As I turn to leave the room, I feel both queasy and grateful on account of the alcohol now boiling and bubbling inside me.

First, I go to the kitchen area where I have been preparing myself food and drink during my stay. Rightfully so, Faith was initially reluctant to let me know the room even existed, but I've gained her trust now. I find a knife which I slide into the side of my waistband and take another just for good measure, which I stick up my sleeve.

Then I head to the control room, the place where I am usually stationed on my rounds as warden. I look around, although I am not feeling particularly afraid, my nerves numbed by the ethanol circulating my veins. I walk towards the complicated-looking panel that I have studied so intensely over the last few days. I find that I am reasonably familiar with it, especially given that it has so many similarities to the controls back at Faith's circus. I guess that, clever as she is, old Faith is a creature of habit. Just like the rest of us.

Just as I am about to tap in the codes for the doors I want to release; an even better idea occurs to me. It's a sick, dark, twisted plot, but it makes the corner of my mouth curl upwards into a sick, dark, twisted grin. It's grotesque and awful in every way imaginable but also sweet and satisfying in equal measure. I let my fingers graze the buttons they are poised above and then think better of it. Instead, I go to the corner of the room where an iron safe hangs on the wall. Fingers trembling with excitement, I clumsily thumb in the code and let out an involuntarily squeak of delight when the door opens with a tiny scrape.

Just ten minutes later, I am walking slowly, as quietly as possible, down the corridor of the ward. The lights are dimmed, and the place is eerily quiet. The usual screeches of pain and bangs of self-destruction that haunt the passage have faded somehow into the atmosphere. Once upon a time, this would have been like the scene from a horror movie to me. Now, it's just another part of life. In fact, I even find myself clamping my teeth together, trying to stifle a childish giggle of excitement as I get closer and closer to my destination.

Is this what insanity feels like?

I scramble to unlock the door using the swipe card. The cell doors can be opened via the security codes, however not without sending an alert to Faith. I learned that thanks to Xenon, whose ugly old lips appear to loosen when a younger, browner bloke offers up sexual favours. While I showered him with compliments and licked his stinking arse hole, he was more than happy to reveal all of his ingenious little tricks set up around the lab. The chump. Should've killed him earlier, probably. But it would have been far too risky, what with the alarm going off at the same time. No… if I have learned anything from Faith and her fucked up ways, it's that patience truly is a virtue. Especially when dealing with a psychopath of this calibre.

When the door opens, the room is automatically flooded with bright grey light triggered by the motion sensor. I push the card back into my pocket and close the door behind me before surveying the contents of the small, gloomy space.

Immediately, I feel a pair of cold eyes latch onto me.

Pig

"Pig!" a voice whispers, the one-syllable word heavily pregnant with hope. It's bittersweet, really. The charming sound of human relief is helplessly buried beneath thick, suffocating layers of the horrific past that the name 'Pig' represents. Gooseflesh ripples up and down my arms. I tingle from head to foot and find myself unable to stand still.

Ahead of me, Daddy is curled up, naked, and covered in filth. Black smudges and streaks of blood stain his body. His ankles and wrists are shackled. He looks like a little boy again, lost and frightened, alone in a terrifying wilderness, hunted by beasts.

"Sh-sh-she killed everyone, Pig," Daddy croaks. His voice rasps as if he has been starved of water. "The whole place... she set fire to them all. Then she..." he swallows and chokes. "She's going to kill us, Pig."

Suddenly, the two figures beside him jerk awake. I turn my attention to them. Inside my trousers, I feel myself harden at the sight. Like Daddy, Dawn and Arlo have been stripped naked and are bound, tied up to a wall like dangerous animals. Their eyes are wide and creased, terrified and exhausted.

"Pig, oh Pig, thank god!" Dawn squeals, tears streaming down her leathery face. "You came. I knew you would. I knew you'd never turn on us."

Arlo struggles in his restraints, then eyes me very seriously, his brow furrowing as he trains his pupils on me. I notice that his ribs are protruding painfully through the skin on his torso as if they are trying to break through. A small pang of sympathy strikes me then as I recall the torturous agony of true hunger. Through my brain, a foggy memory crispens and replays. The stench of shit and stale blood rife in my nostrils, my skin clammy as I lay on my side, hunched over. Gripping tightly onto my grumbling belly as starvation pains radiate through my entire skeleton. Fighting through a thick throng of other filthy, afraid beings, just to slurp a filthy concoction of gruel and saliva from a trowel.

Like an animal.

Then, once I have ingested that small, revolting scrap of sustenance, collapsing onto my side with acidic tears pricking my eyes. Seeing a tall, mean-looking figure standing over me. Being spat on and kicked so hard in the gut so that my vision blurs and my head spins.

Even though it was such a long time ago, the figure's face is as clear and sharp as day to me.

And now, I stare right back at that very same face.

Oh, but how the roles have reversed.

"Pig," breathes Arlo sharply. But his once intimidating boom of a voice is raspy, undermined now by his feeble, helpless appearance.

I blink.

Take a sharp intake of breath.

Blood pulses in my eardrums like the deafening roar of an insatiable beast.

My lip curls upwards into a dark smile.

"What?" I challenge, all at once savouring the rush of endorphins flooding my system. Years and years-worth of helplessness disintegrates in these short, fatal moments. I feel like I'm growing, surging upwards so that I tower above these weak, pathetic individuals.

The power, at last, is in my hands.

"Pig? What are you doing? Why aren't you helping us?" breathes Dawn, clutching at the chain that binds her neck. Her eyes are wide, pleading… begging.

"Sorry," I hear myself say faintly. "Let me get you out of those chains." As if I'm in a trance, my body moves without any conscious direction from my brain. I sense myself removing the knife and brandishing it. Dawn's face softens in gratitude. Daddy, however, scurries backwards, his face wide with shock as it occurs to him how incredibly and utterly fucked they all are.

"I don't think that'll cut through," Dawn says, examining the shackles and sniffing, oblivious to the blood-thirsty glint in my eyes.

"Don't hurt her, please don't hurt her," Daddy begins to cry like a pathetic little kid. "I'm sorry. I'm sorry for whatever has happened in the past."

A sudden, shrill screech of a laugh escapes my lips.

Doesn't he know?

Doesn't he realise?

That it's just. Too. Fucking. Late.

I lurch forward in a frenzy, jabbing the blade manically through the air at no target in particular. When its edge meets flesh, a warm blood splatter drenches my cheeks, and the sound of Dawn's croaky screams drown out the sound of slashing.

She's pretty much dead in an instant, reduced to a spluttering, choking fountain of scarlet within seconds. But I keep going. I keep pulling back my wrist and thrusting it into her, breaking apart every inch of that creased, leathery skin. I keep going until I feel her frail bones splinter and see her severed arteries pop and explode. I keep going until she is reduced from barely human to nothing but a liquid lump of saturated meat.

"NOOOOOO!" screeches Daddy, suddenly shocking me back into the moment.

I blink.

I'm on my knees.

My skin itches, irritated by the thin coating of human fluid.

The knife slips from my hand and clatters onto the ground.

"WHY? WHAT THE FUCK?" sobs Daddy, burying his head into his hands. His entire body heaves and rocks. I almost feel sorry for him.

"Exactly… *exactly*…" I mutter, shaking my head, licking the iron tang of blood from my lips. "Why? Why did any of this ever have to happen?" I look up at him. Cock my head. Piss dribbles from the end of his shrivelled, flaccid cock, and pools around his filthy feet.

"Fucking pitiful."

A gruff, fearless voice causes me to spin around. Instinctively, I grab hold of the knife and hold it up. Embarrassingly, my wrist trembles and shakes, betraying the fear that still courses through my veins for him.

"Shut the fuck up," I force myself to command him, palm sweaty on the hilt of the knife.

Arlo chuckles. Sits back, holds his head backwards so that his face is facing the ceiling. He closes his eyes like he is relaxing on a sun lounger a million miles away from here. I find myself, even in spite of things, filled with envy for him. It consumes me like poison.

"It really took you all this time to finally stand up to me?" Arlo muses. "You've had all these years, dude. You could have stabbed me in my sleep. Could have set us all on fire. Shit, you could have taken one of the fucking cars and ratted us out to the police. Not those corrupt fuckers by the farm, but the big guns."

His words sting like a slap around the face.

"But you waited. You *wasted* your whole life, man..." he smirks, then lets out a small, satisfied sigh. "The way I see it, you deserved all of this. Every single last bit of it."

I collapse, suddenly overwhelmed with grief.

"We took your life from you," Arlo tells me gleefully. "Stole it. Easy as pie. Forced you to work for us. Treated you like shit on a pig farm... you *helped* us. Do you get that? You actually *helped* us make money off of killing and stealing," he laughs even louder.

Thick tears of sorrow plug up my eyes.

"You want to know what I did to your girlfriend?" he whispers.

I shake my head slightly, unable to move or cry out on account of the pure, paralysing devastation that has taken hold of me.

"Abdul?"

My eyes snap open. Hearing my old name... it's like a portal to the past.

"Before we killed her, we took turns on her," Arlo cackles hysterically. "I took her in the arse whilst River fucked her till she bled. We passed her around the boys, then strung her up on a meat hook through her cunt... nearly killed her. But we weren't done. We had plenty more playing to do. Slashed off her tits, yanked out her teeth, and pulled off her nails. It was hard work and very messy."

I can't help but envision the horrific scene. Prue's petite body struggling, her mouth open whilst she gasped for help that was never going to come. I huddle over and cry like a baby, wishing more than anything that I had been killed on that day too.

"And what did you do?" Arlo quips. Another cold, sharp laugh of pure evil. "You fucking rolled our joints for us. You helped us. You've been with us, *one of us,* for all these years. And it takes us being locked up for you to finally get revenge? That is the most pathetic, weakest shit I've ever heard."

I taste fresh blood and realise my teeth are piercing the inside of my mouth.

"Kill me," Arlo groans, half bemused, half in emotional turmoil.

I picture the burning building and imagine his young kids burning within its walls. I imagine their flesh melting, their little jaws wide open as they scream and scream for their daddy.

"No," I finally respond. Wiping my tears with the back of my sleeve, I stand up. I tower over him and force myself to meet his eye, to savour the pain and grief shining in his icy irises. "I won't kill you."

Arlo's face drops, and he stares up at me in bewilderment. I see the tiny flicker of hope in his iris and realise that this is what it must have been like for him all of those times that he was in control. Looking down on weak, defenceless captives, seeing the pure pain, terror, and tiny glimmer of doubt smeared across their pathetic faces.

"Abdul..." he breathes out, his jaw falling open to reveal yellowing teeth rotting from years of drug use. "I... I'm sorry."

"Me too," I whisper, clenching my fist hard around the knife. My arm trembles, suddenly filled with fresh energy. I step forward, lift my foot and stomp down hard on his naked knee cap. A horrific crack fills the air and appears to echo, the noise laced with his scream of agony. Before he can catch his breath, I repeat the brutal movement on his other leg, rendering the sick piece of shit immobile.

"I didn't do anything because you fucked me up," I snarl, sinking down to my knees and pushing my face up close to his stinking, screaming mouth. "I'm not the same man I was all those years ago. You've infected me with your disease. I'm tainted meat. Just as sick and fucked up in the head as you."

He spits at me but fails in his suffering. A weak, blood-spotted trail of drool drips from his lip and hangs in a grotesque paste from his chin.

"Maybe I wouldn't have had it in me before...." I hiss, "but I sure as hell do now. What was it you said you did to Prue?"

His entire body stops. Clenches. Freezes still.

I force his disabled legs apart and position the knife down beneath his balls at the entrance of his rectum. "Hung her up on a meat hook...." I grimace, "by her *cunt?*" I spit out the foul, disgusting word like it is a decomposing rat stuck down my throat.

My worst nightmare... my sworn enemy... the man who destroyed my life, writhes and squirms in front of me, his face red and wrinkled like a disgruntled newborn.

"Please...no..." he gasps.

I swallow back fresh tears.

"That's what we said to you," I say slowly, before ramming the point of the knife hard up into his anal orifice. There is a loud, satisfying POP and a warm gush of torrential blood as his innards begin to leak out. He screams, continuing to twist and turn his body in what I can only imagine must be true, pure agony. Although, I don't finish him off. Instead, I stand up and take a look at my handy work as if I have just finished creating a masterpiece. A canvas of sickly, drug-mottled flesh leaking jets and dribbles of blood.

For a brief moment, I consider putting Daddy out of his misery. I don't look at him- I'm too transfixed, too entranced by the sight of Arlo bleeding out from his genitals. However, I can sense the sheer horror radiating off of him from his corner, where he cowers and whimpers.

I have become very good at detecting fear.

After all, does the kid really deserve to die here beside his mother's bloody, mutilated carcass, whilst his father figure screams and cries like a weak little bitch?

But in the end, I just shrug and laugh it off.

"No one ever gave me any fucking mercy," I mutter before turning on my heel and marching back to the control panel fast and with urgency I did not possess before. As I steel back down the corridor, I kick and pound at the doors of the other rooms.

"I'M RELEASING THE DOORS!" I bark at the top of my lungs before breaking out into a jog and hurrying back to my station. Heart pounding, I place my palm above the door, panting with the exhilaration, tingling from head to toe with anticipation of the madness that is sure to ensue.

"What the fuck are you doing?"

I spin around to see Xenon standing behind me in the doorway, still wearing his usual lab attire as if he has been sleeping in it. In his hands, he carries a shotgun. Suddenly, my blood-stained kitchen knife no longer feels like the hard-core killing device that it was just ten seconds ago.

His beady rat eyes squint and flit to the screens behind me, presumably drawn to the bright flash of red now highlighting Arlo's cell. Even though they are muted, the sound of Daddy's cries ring sharply through the air like a siren.

"What is going on here?" he asks incredulously, taking a step forward and holding up the gun. "I'm getting Faith…."

"No," I interrupt, moving towards him. "There's no need for that. Honestly…" I clear my throat in an attempt to look nervous, "come on. You must know what she gets like when she's angry. I just lost control, but there's no need to upset Faith over it, right? It'll just make it hell to work for her for a week, right?"

He cocks his head and contemplates this. "Losing control is getting fucked up down the pub or screwing your wife's sister. *That…*" he jabs a finger behind me at the camera screen, "… Jesus Christ…" he lets out a low, wheezy laugh and shakes his head. "You're dead meat. She was saving the woman to trial some new drug addiction therapy."

"Xenon, come on, we're friends, right?"

He scowls at me.

"Co-workers," I insist. A bead of sweat trickles down the back of my neck as I notice him delve into his pocket for his phone. "Faith will take it out on both of us…."

"I doubt it," Xenon says, "I'm irreplaceable. But there's a million more of you where you came from." He smirks his lip curling upward in a disgusting, ugly smile. "Should've stayed in your own country, pal. Bet you wish you had."

I almost laugh at the ridiculousness of it. A racial slur from an ugly psychopath at a time like this feels like a baby ant nibbling at my ankle. Before he can say another word, I turn back to the control panel and hit the button. The siren is activated, and there is a loud moan as all of the doors in the corridor creak open.

An earth-shattering bang fills my ears, causing my brain to rattle and vibrate inside my skull. Warmth spreads from somewhere on my body, and I look down and notice the blood. For some reason, my face relaxes into a smile.

I've been shot, and soon I will be dead.

I'm not afraid.

Hope

I keep glancing at the clock. It's late. I know in my mind that realistically, the person I now know is called Abdul should have had enough time to do... *something*. But there have been no alerts. No signs. I debate telling Mum everything, say that we have to use her emergency escape plan right this second before the authorities find out. But, in front of the TV, the cartoons illuminating her face, she looks so at peace. Apparently oblivious that I've betrayed her.

"I want to talk," I blurt out before I can stop myself.

From the other room, I hear Beau shriek and laugh, then Mischa sigh and say something. It would have been better if Mischa had stayed at the lab to help Abdul, but Mum is still in two minds about trusting her. So, instead, Mischa came home with us to babysit Beau whilst Mother, and I bond.

"About what, darling?" Mum asks, turning to me with a look of innocence splashed across her face. In the darkness, she looks terrifying.

"I want to know about the farm," I say. It's only half true. "And the circus, and the lab."

If she is shocked, she does a good job of hiding it. She smiles sweetly and nods as if we are having a perfectly normal, totally mundane conversation about everyday life. She licks her lips whilst she lights a spliff and holds it in the corner of her mouth. "What is it that you want to know?"

"Do you really kill people, Mum?"

She inhales deeply, her eyelids closing as she absent-mindedly holds out the joint to me. I ignore it.

"You do, don't you?"

Mum laughs and takes another drag. Still, she keeps her eyes firmly closed. "I came to this earth with a job, Hope. And you can't even begin to imagine how much I have achieved."

"Money?" I probe, "is that what this is all about? Getting money out of other people's suffering?"

At that, her eyes snap open, and she shoots me a glare of frustration. "Don't be so ignorant," she spits as if the words are disgusting on the tip of her tongue. "Don't you know me at all? And besides, I never saw you judging when you were helping me scrape dead meat off the ground...."

My fists clench, anger boiling beneath my skin. "Because you made me think it was all Beau. You made me think that my disabled older sister would be locked away."

Mum snorts, "she *would* be, Hope. Don't you see? No space on this earth for the weak. No room for poor, defenceless souls."

I watch a slim flash of vulnerability cross her face. It's so brief, so fleeting that I barely even register it. But it's so strong that I feel it in my soul. Hard.

"Is that what you were?" I whisper. Somehow, the room seems even darker, regardless of the dumb cartoons flashing about on the television screen. "Someone hurt you, so now you hurt people."

"I don't want to hurt anyone," she says quietly, bringing the joint to her lips again. "I want to help people. I want to change the world. How many other people would exclusively hire disabled people? Or turn around the lives of pathetic druggies?"

My heart lowers in my chest. "But you can do that without killing people, Mum," I say softly.

She laughs, "I could hurt animals instead," she says sarcastically, resentment strangling her voice. "Innocent, simple-minded animals that don't even know how to betray or neglect. Superior by innocence."

"What you are doing is wrong, Mum," I tell her. "All those people... what if they have daughters just like Beau and me? You're taking their life and playing God."

The silence is as loud and deafening as a gunshot. My heart skips a beat. I feel sweat prickle on the back of my neck, and a shiver rushes down my spine like a million tiny bugs.

"I *am* God," she says suddenly, tossing away the joint. She steps on it with her barefoot, apparently oblivious to the painful hiss of the butt on her flesh. Suddenly, she towers above me like a mountain, leering down at me like a lion about to gobble up a juicy rodent. "I'm untouchable," she hisses, more like an angry cat than a human.

"If you're so untouchable, then why am I about to bring you down?" I ask her, my voice thick with a buried sob. I want to stand up but find myself glued to the seat, all of my limbs heavy. Instead, I push my hand behind my back, and my fingers search for the hilt of the knife behind me.

She gasps as if she has been winded. Her face crumples.

"But... I made you...."

"Just say you'll stop," I croak, the tears now streaming down my cheeks. "Say you're done with it. I'll run away with you and Beau. The escape plan you always used to talk about... I know now it must be real."

Mum clutches at her cheeks, her skin turning a clammy white. "Not you, Hope. Anyone but you...."

I swallow and force myself to stand up. I raise my voice, trying to sound stronger than I feel. "You always said you'd do anything for Beau and me. Well, now is your chance to prove yourself. Let's just go away. Make a new start."

My mother steps forward. I tighten my grip on the knife's handle, my heart thundering dangerously fast inside my rib cage.

"My mother abused me as a child," she whispers softly. As soon as she musters the words, I sense a weight rising quickly off of her shoulders. "Only had me as leverage. She was a prostitute, blackmailing this guy, my dad. Rinsed him for all he had, just so she would never tell his wife."

"We lived on a farm. She had boyfriends around a lot. They found it funny to kick me around, make me sleep out in the pigpen. I was barely even four years old."

"Oh, Mum..." I sigh, rushing forwards and engulfing her in my arms. She hugs me back tightly, but her slim figure feels limp and ghostly in my embrace.

"That wasn't the worst part, though," she continues. "I got a little brother..." although I can't see her face, I can tell by her voice that she is smiling at his memory.

"Uncle Sundance?"

"No. To be honest, I can't remember his name. For so many years, I tried to pretend that Sundance was him... after he..." she chokes, splutters. "He died."

"How?"

"He was just a baby," she moans in a low voice, a tone that is so heavily pregnant with pain that I barely even recognise it as my mother's. "And I did everything for him. But one day I… I wasn't there. And my mother was fucked up again, pissing about in the slaughterhouse with her latest boyfriend. They fucking killed him."

Fresh tears sting my eyes.

"They killed him. Then they ground him up like cow flesh being minced. I walked in to find my baby brother, the only human in the entire world I had ever loved, had been ripped apart and shredded. His little body barely even recognisable."

Silence as she cries quietly into the crook of my shoulder.

"I'm so sorry, Mum."

I feel her body tense and stiffen like a corpse.

"Karma," she whispers simply. "They all got what was coming to them. In the end, we all do."

For a few moments, we just stand there, holding on to each other.

She continues to sniffle.

It's eerie.

Bone-chilling to hear my own mother cry. Almost like a foreshadowing, that everything I have ever known is shortly about to come crashing down on top of me.

"Mum, we've got to go," I tell her, gently pushing her away so that I can look into her deep green eyes. "It's over. The police will be here soon. I want us to get out. I know you can do it. We have enough money. Don't we?"

Her expression hardens.

"Why do we have to go?" she asks me, her weepy voice suddenly replaced by a sharp knife's edge. "What have you done, Hope?"

Goose flesh ripples over my skin. My stomach drops.

"Just trust me," I plead.

Mum laughs, throws her head back, and cackles like a wicked witch. I freeze, temporarily rendered rigid by how utterly terrifying she looks in the shadows.

"Mum…" I begin, "Mum, I…" before I can say another word, she's on me, crashing down upon me so that my shoulder blades crack against the floor. I open my mouth to scream, but she slaps her hand to my lips.

"What have you done, Hope? Teamed up with... Pig?" she spits, her saliva erupting everywhere, spattering my sweat-drenched skin. "Going against your mother, huh?" she laughs again, lowering her hands from my mouth and clenching my throat. "Oh, the irony," she chuckles, a tear leaking from the corner of her eye. "All these followers... all these people who loved me, worshipped me. Would kill or die for me. The only ones who wouldn't? My own parents and my only biological child."

I choke. Inside my right hand, I still feel the knife, but everything inside my body screams at me not to use it. Her face is starting to blur, and the world is beginning to fade. I know that if I don't do something now, I'm about to be murdered by my own mother.

And worse still, she will get away with it.

She'll use my corpse to complete her cure for cancer and earn even more money and even more fame and notoriety off of me.

Somehow, she'll do it.

With the last tiny shred of life still pumping through my veins, I lunge upwards and shove the knife sideways into my own mother's side. At once, she screams, a piercing, ungodly noise that makes me feel like the entire world is ending. Whilst she's distracted by her pain, I grab her shoulders and throw her to the ground, leaping on top of her, suddenly alive with the electricity and adrenaline.

Warm blood gushes over my hand, and my high soon crashes into deep, dark misery. Blood sputters from my mother's lips, and I realise she's dying.

"Mama?"

I look up. Beau is standing in the hallway, blocking all light, her face illuminated by the cartoons still dancing on the television screen. At first, her face is dull with confusion but soon contorts with that horrifically familiar anger that I have grown to know so well. Her eyes narrow, turning jet black, glittering as she pounces on me, roughly throwing me onto the ground beside our mother.

Before I can register what is happening, a sharp, blinding agony takes over my right shoulder. A scream catches in my throat, ripping through my vocal chords like a nightmare. Through the blinding pain, flashes of reality force their way through the front of my skull; the horrific image emblazoned forever more on my brain.

My sister gnaws at my flesh like an animal, only coming up for air when her mouth is filled with shredded, bloodied muscle. Her dreadful canines tear through the raw meat just inches above my face so that spurts of my own hot blood leaks all over my face. My jaw is open, fixed tight. I am still. Not even breathing, as I feel my own sister eat me alive. Over her ravenous jaws snapping, I hear my mother wail. I catch a flash of her over Beau's shoulder and see that she has somehow staggered to her feet and is now standing over us, watching in despair.

I expect my mother, in spite of everything, to fight her off. To haul me out of the murky depths of death I find myself sinking so quickly into.

But instead, she just watches. I reach out a hand or at least try to.

But Mother is too distant. Too far away to help.

Mischa

Shit.

Fuck.

"Oh my... oh my fucking god!" I yelp before I can stop myself, my voice wobbling as if dangling precariously from a tight rope like a circus performer. I cling on to the clammy doorway with my sweating palms, the bones inside shuddering as I attempt to steady myself. But neither Faith nor Beau seems to notice me, both irresponsive to my squeak of fear.

Even in the darkness, I can sense the blood. I can smell it. Taste it, even suffocating me from the inside. In the gloom of the living room, it looks like a shiny black goo, saturating every inch of the floor. It creeps up the walls. It buries Hope's lifeless body deeper and deeper, the mass of it expanding by the second.

Crying hopelessly, I spot the flash of a knife lying discarded to my right. My eyes flit upwards again to the awful sight, where Beau's monstrous frame straddles the teenager, her ferocious face growling like something conceived in hell. Beside them, Faith is standing upright, distracted by the terrifying din. She has her back to me, her shadow somehow thinner, weaker than I first thought. Like a helpless child cowering in the dark.

My feet move before I even have a chance to consciously think. I reach down for the knife, suddenly no longer trembling. Beau roars again before lunging down for more. The pit of my stomach churns at the heightened squelches and grunts of her devouring flesh and slurping blood. Yet somehow, the awful soundtrack spurs me on. I see the scene- the mother and her two daughters- through tunnel vision, framed now with black. I'm no longer a person, afraid and uncertain, grieving for a dead man and the mediocre yet contented way my life used to be. I'm just a thing. A piece of the game. And I am about to make the most crucial move. A move that no one has yet dared to play. A move that will end this sick, twisted game. Forever.

When I'm close enough, my knees feel like jelly. I'm drunk on the intoxicating rush of chemicals surging through my arteries. I slam the point of the knife down hard, plunging it quickly through the chilling air. It meets the crouched, solid wall of Beau's back, sending a surge of pain shooting up my arm on impact. I force myself to lift it again and repeat the motion, harder this time. The scoffing noises stop and are replaced by a horrendous shriek of pain. Beau jerks upright, sending the hilt of the knife flying from my palm. Her sudden movement knocks me onto my behind, and I scramble backwards on wiry limbs that begin to feel numb with terror. The giant turns. The light from the blaring television shines on her, illuminating horrific, deformed features. They contort madly through the curtain of blood and entrails smeared across them, her pitch-black eyes opening and shutting so rapidly that she looks like a crazed animatronic.

At first, I freeze. My feet and palms are welded to the spot where I am sprawled on the wet, sticky ground. I know that I'm about to die. In the background, I see Hope's mutilated face, lifeless and ripped apart as easily as a flimsy piece of paper.

A reminder of my own fate.

I prepare for Beau to lunge for me, to pin me down, and eat me alive. I will myself to shut my eyes, but something keeps them wide open, stinging with tears.

But instead, she produces a loud, long, carnivorous roar and sinks down to her knees with an almighty crash.

She collapses, almost in slow motion, to the ground.

Head down in her little sister's

"What the hell did you do?"

I'd forgotten about Faith, temporarily.

I gasp, snapping my head towards the wide-mouthed woman whose gaunt, ghostly frame towers high above me, bloodshot eyes pulsating from their socket, illuminated by the flashes of television light. It takes one wobbly step forward for me to break out of my stupor. I scrabble backwards like a crab, my fingers searching desperately on the sticky, darkened floor for the blade. As Faith charges forward, I see the trails of blood leaking from her lips and the wound bleeding on her torso.

Before she pounces on me, I jump to my feet, leaving the knife behind as I make my frantic escape. Salty tears blind me, making navigating the tight, unfamiliar maze of the house blur and close in all around me from a million different angles. My heart is pounding but not loud enough to drown out the rough, staggered footsteps of my captor behind me. Her breath expels from her lips like a scream, long and high-pitched enough to make my blood curdle in my veins.

"JUST FUCK OFF!" I scream, quickening my pace so that I'm beating the floor with my feet. Sweat dribbles from my brow, congealing with blood spatter that tastes like stale rust on my lower lip.

Behind me, I hear Faith cackle through her distressed pants.

Fucking crazy bitch.

In a stampede of emotion, I cascade down the hall and through the arch of the kitchen, where I briefly pause behind the marble breakfast bar. I blink furiously, cramming myself against a crevice in a wall. I know Faith is weakening, the blood draining quickly from her, but still, I hear her excited pants just a few metres away. I furiously scan the room, searching for a knife block, which I spot on one of the luxuriously-tiled sides.

Empty.

I hurry over to it, just in case, only to find that my first suspicions are confirmed.

All of the blades have been removed.

"Little Pig, Little Pig…" I hear Faith wheeze before spluttering. Her ghostly pale face appears in the doorway, then a raised bloody hand gripping tightly onto the hilt of a larger, more severe-looking knife. My stomach drops.

"Just leave me alone…." I croak, throat closing in on itself. My head spins, body trembling all over. I think that there is another entrance to the kitchen, but I find that my feet have turned into lead blocks, making every movement slow and impossible.

Like in some sort of twisted nightmare, Faith gets a kick out of my fear. Feeds on it like a hungry leech sucking blood, gaining strength with every pint of scarlet body fluid. She advances on me quicker than expected, in spite of the nasty slash to her mid-section. She holds the knife well as if she has done it a million times, the edge of the blade held up as if it is being aimed directly at me.

Trapped and desperate, I start opening cupboards, tossing out anything I can find, hurling them across the room. Almost everything I throw at her misses. It's like even the house is possessed by her. Damned to perform her evil deeds. As she approaches, laughing and wheezing, manic and wide-eyed, I dash further back and stop just in front of the kettle.

The kettle.

Just before all of the ruckus between Faith and Hope, I'd been about to make myself up one of those herbal teas. I didn't give a fuck if it contained opiates or some hyperactive form of cannabis. I just needed to be numb. But I'd never gotten the chance anyway because Beau had galloped off like some killer equestrian and began eating Hope alive.

A faint wisp of smoke quivers above the spout. I know that it is filled to the brim.

Without a second thought, I grab the handle and spin around to face Faith, who is slashing the knife playfully in the air in front of her. She doesn't seem to notice my new choice of weapon, evidently too wrapped up in whatever psychotic joke was causing her to project such evil, horrific sniggers.

"I said, fuck *off.*" I open the lid of the kettle and splash the contents over her. Instantly, the boiling liquid hisses in protest against her bruised and bloodied flesh, and the metal knife in her hand clatters to the floor, defeated.

She does not scream, instead sucks in a long, high-pitched breath and clamps her rapidly reddening hands over her face. I stagger backwards clumsily and dump the kettle and its remaining contents onto the kitchen side.

"Oh shit, oh shit, oh shit...." I hear myself mutter over and over again as if the words will somehow calm the chaotic roaring in my eardrums.

Faith sinks down onto her knees, the bones cracking against tile. I wince at the sight of the horrific, scarlet red and purple blisters quickly forming on the surface of her skin. She breathes out slowly, deeply, like a labouring mother panting through contractions. Slowly, she lowers herself so that she is laying down on her side, nothing but a weak, feeble being, reminiscent of a foetus on the soiled floor.

I watch her for far too long. I've no idea how many seconds or minutes go past as I take in her broken, shrivelled body and almost marvel at the irony. My hero. My goal. My idol.

Dying.

At my own hand.

When she makes an unexpected jerk and moves one of her palms slightly to reveal a grossly deformed eyebrow- the flesh melted by the scorching liquid, I move.

Before she can do anything else, I scramble to the floor and snatch up the knife, which lies in a now cool pool of liquid. My wrist shakes underneath its weight, and I hold it protectively to my chest, facing outwards in a threat at my enemy.

Then, I wait.

I wait until, finally, Faith lets out a small, human moan of pain. My body tenses up, and I instinctively get up onto my haunches, ready to pounce if need be.

"I'm not going to die," she mumbles, immediately hissing afterwards as if even words tumbling from her mouth are excruciating. "I won't. I… I'm God."

A surge of white-hot anger grips me by the throat with an iron fist. My brow furrows, and I jab the knife closer in the air towards her so that she can sense the point of the blade.

"You're not a fucking God, Faith," I whisper. "You're the devil. No, you're worse." I swallow back a lump of sadness that chokes me every time I think of Jace. My jaw grits together. I will not cry again today.

"At least the devil knows he's an arsehole," I tell her, raising my voice. "At least the devil knows he is evil. You're the most evil…." I sputter, trying to wrap my head around it all, "…the evilest *thing* I have ever heard of. More evil than cancer, more evil than war, more evil than any serial killer, murderer, or psychopath…."

She cuts me off, abruptly removing both hands from her face. She exposes the pink and red, doughy, swollen mound of flesh that shines painfully raw where her features used to be. Involuntarily, I let out a shriek of horror and almost drop the knife all over again through my shock. Edges of her face are swollen, deformed, painfully twisted, and contorted into the face of a monster. The light ahead shines directly down on her, illuminating the glossiest points of her agonising wounds. Just like she's an experiment, stretched out on the lab table.

"You really are a stupid fucking cunt, aren't you?" hisses Faith. She remains horizontal, but her eyes blaze up at me like a portal to hell. "There's no such thing as evil. This world is fucking evil. And we are just the mindless pawns playing into its sick, twisted narrative. Me, on the other hand," she laughs. "I have made a difference. I'm saving animals. I'm purging all the evil, ignorant cretins that they die for."

I furiously blink back tears. I will not cry.

"And at what cost, Faith?" I question her, my voice just inches from breaking apart. "Both of your daughters are dead. Is your life even worth living anymore?"

I recoil the moment I have said it, instant regret falling over me like a slow showering of dust.

But Faith does not move. There is no physical retaliation. No sudden surge of strength where she bends the knife from my hand and brutally stabs me to my demise.

Then, somewhere else.

I hear it.

A low, grotesque grunt followed by slippery pants and snorts.

The heavy, intimidating slam of unsteady footsteps.

"Mummy...."

I freeze.

Pig

A long time ago, before all of this, I was one of those typical, naïve romantics who believed in fate. What is meant to be will be. Our actions, in the grand scheme of things, don't matter a damn thing because there is already a plan for each and every one of us.

Then, I got captured, torn from my charmed life, and plummeted headfirst onto the farm, where the bright, promising glow of my future was promptly snuffed. For so many years, I agonised over why the fuck I went on that trip. Because I wanted to get to know Prue. But we both hated Kevin, our boss, so why the hell didn't I just get over my stupid pride and ask her out on a date? I became convinced that fate was nothing but a fallacy, and every single second, of every minute, of every hour, of every day, counted. Every split choice, every word, every step was creating another swerve on the path of life.

Now, I don't have a fucking clue.

Pain takes over the entirety of my right calf and ebbs upwards into my thigh and pelvis. My chest burns as I pant with effort, dragging my wounded leg along behind me as I let myself out of the lab and out into the cool night air outside. I glance down and can't help but grimace at the sight of the sodden, blood-drenched shirt wrapped crudely around the injury. In my hand, the sharp ridges of Xenon's car key rub up against my clammy palm. My brain is still a war zone, battling out the options as I stagger towards the car as quickly as possible, nearly toppling over like a domino on multiple occasions.

Risk finding a police station? Only to find that they're as corrupt as the other forces that played into Faith's sick, twisted games?

Or go back to Faith's house? Only to find that she has killed Mischa and Hope and is ready and waiting to capture and torture me just the same.

Of course, neither idea sounds appealing. Both images in my head send a grotesque shiver rushing down my spine.

As I finally find Xenon's small, ugly-looking smart car, I half-collapse against the driver's door, wheezing and spluttering as I try to catch my breath. When I've calmed myself, I pat up and down my good leg, feeling out the canvas pockets of my trouser. The solid, comforting bulge of the gun greets my fingertips, and I breathe out a sigh of relief. I get a fresh bout of energy and get inside the car.

Driving along the dark, inadequately-lit country roads, flashes of Xenon streak across my vision like thunderbolts illuminating a cloudy sky. Every fleeting memory of the sight, the smell, the sound of it no longer disturbs me. Instead, it feels like a hit. An injection of pure joy and manic amusement.

He shot me, and I fell. I thought I was dying. But the stupid prick had missed my torso. Clearly had no proper experience with a gun.

Very shoddy work on Faith's part.

Not only that, but the force from the bullet had blown him backwards on impact, causing the gun to clatter onto the ground and his skinny, slimy frame to tip over backwards.

In his surprise, and in spite of my pain, I'd lunged forwards, scooping up the weapon as swiftly and effectively as if I had been practising my entire life.

The memory causes the splatters of Xenon's blood showering my face to prickle and tingle. A warm reminder that the fucker is dead, and *I* am responsible.

Maybe I do believe in fate after all. Maybe I was put on this earth to wipe out every single one of these twisted freaks. The universe just needed them all brought together. Arlo, Dawn, Xenon, Daddy…all tied together by one common thread.

A thread that I am about to sever.

At the last minute, I decide to make an abrupt turn in the road, the tyres screeching loudly in my tired ears.

For the first time in a long time, I let myself think about Prue. I dare to let my mind travel towards that dark, shadowy corner where jaded clips of the future we could have had swirl sadly in their tight confines. Tears stream down both of my cheeks as I picture her face, and my hands instinctively clamp around the wheel like vices.

It's time, Abdul.

I whimper as the sound of her voice tinkles in my head like the rattling of little glasses clinking against one another. "Time for what?" I whisper to myself, blinking away tears.

You know.

My foot presses harder on the gas, and my brow furrows into a deep frown of concentration. I do know. It's time to put an end to this madness, once and for all.

And if I'm captured, strung up, and slaughtered like a pig in the process, then so be it.

God loves a trier.

Goose flesh runs up and down my arms. I speed down the dangerously dark lane until the familiar opening towards Faith's new place comes into view. From the outside, it looks dark. There is a trickle of light from somewhere deeper inside the house, but the front windows are black. Heart palpitations thunder painfully in my throat and vibrate in my eardrums. A sickly ache begins to pound at the forefront of my skull.

It just spurs me on further.

I drive further away so that I am not directly in front of the building. Just because I've been submissive for all these years doesn't mean I've not caught on to a few evil tricks. I was passive but observant. Remain hidden for as long as possible. The element of surprise can be anybody's most powerful secret weapon.

I stop the car, not bothering to park it straight. Even if I wanted to, my hands are shaking too much, my leg growing deader by the second as I lose more blood. My muscles groan in protest as I reach over into the footwell of the passenger seat and haul out a rucksack. I know that I need to get to a hospital if I want even a sliver of a chance at survival, but survival is now no longer the priority.

"Come on," I grumble beneath my breath, yanking the bag towards me, then opening up the car door and stepping out onto the lamp-lit pavement.

Up above me, a full white moon illuminates the navy blanket of night. A shiver runs down my spine. Makes me think of wolves. Except, I tell myself with perhaps too much confidence, tonight I do not fear the wolves. In a hideously cringy moment, I mutter to myself, "I *am* the motherfucking wolf."

With Hope's door key that she smuggled to me earlier, I slip in easily through the back gate, instantly triggering off a white blaze of fairy lights on auto setting. I halt, freezing instantly, blinking in the headlights like a small, weak animal. Then, I wait. I wait for some big burly nightmare of a henchman to come running at me with a harpoon or something equally as absurd. Or for Beau to creep out from nowhere and consume me whole like some land-roaming whale. Or, maybe, it would be Faith herself, shooting me in the knee cap so that I'm rendered immobile, then leaving me to die a slow, torturous death on the cold, hard ground.

But no one comes. I prick my ears for noise but hear nothing but the sounds of a night-time bird fluttering in a tree somewhere. It's eerily silent. As though the walls of the home have been built to be soundproof.

I slink around the outskirts of the garden, trying to gauge where the back door is. My heart skips a beat when I see that it is slightly ajar, and I realise that there must be somebody just inside. I drop, unzip the rucksack and remove the gun that I used to blow Xenon's big old brains out. When I told it, the stench of dead man's blood stings my nostrils. I shiver with pleasure as the aroma hits me.

Slinging the rucksack back over my shoulder, I creep further along the path, aiming the barrel of the gun ahead. Warm liquid spills from the sodden rags covering my leg, and I hear it trickling against the paving stones with every movement.

When I was training to be head of HR, all those years ago, before the farm, my mentor told me it was always best to take a diplomatic approach. Address and conquer one problem at a time, and the rest will gradually fall into place, like the sliding pieces of a jigsaw puzzle. I apply that here.

One mission.

One focus.
Kill Faith.
And *anyone* who tries to stand in my way.

Hope

I feel high, but not in a good way.

It's the kind of high when you've made the fatal error of smoking weed after drinking alcohol. You feel sick. Out of touch. Out of control.

I'm weak, shaking from head to toe like a leaf in a rainstorm. The darkness swims and jitters all around me like a broken videotape, and for a moment, I genuinely wonder if I have died. I cough, rusty-tasting phlegm erupting from the back of my throat as my chest heaves. I sit up and instinctively touch my forehead as gravity seems to spin again.

"Help," I wheeze, but the noise takes everything out of me, and I need to lay back down. I feel blood on me and in me, clinging to my insides and suffocating me internally. All around me, it is dark, the television screen finally nothing but an extension of the pitch-black nothingness that surrounds me.

Me, me, me, me.

Me.

As I lay there, barely strong enough to even breathe, I wonder how different things might have been if I hadn't been so fucking wrapped up in myself for all these years. Maybe if I'd been as thoughtful as Mischa, or as brave as Abdul, or as smart as my own mother, I'd have seen all of this from miles and miles off.

Maybe I could have made a difference.

I blink up at the gloomy abyss of the ceiling and try to imagine myself floating upwards out of life and out of consciousness. But no matter how hard I think of it, it doesn't happen.

I am still, painfully, very much alive.

But why?

I sense a flicker of movement in the doorway. I snap my head to look and blink into the darkness, but I cannot make out a figure. My buttocks tenses as I envision Beau plunging herself at me again, ready to finally finish off the job she started earlier.

Then again, Beau is probably full up by now.
And tired.

I listened to Mischa's deafening screams earlier as they rattled through the bones of the house like a horrific nightmare. Worse still, I listened to them gradually fade and die, as I imagined my big sister ripping her heart out and sucking it dry like a red strawberry lollipop.

I open my mouth to speak, and an involuntary gurgle of blood drips from my throat alongside a louder-than-intended croak. Instinctively, my hand twitches and falls in an attempt to reach my struggling chest, but I'm far too weak for so much movement.
Footsteps. Breaths.
Then, a voice.
"Hope?" a deep, husky voice whispers into the still air.
"Abdul," I mumble, more blood pooling at the top of my throat. "Help," I struggle to muster through the rusted liquid that blocks my airway. "Police," I wheeze, ingesting another vile mouthful of blood-spotted phlegm.
To my alarm, he doesn't move, just stays hovering above me. Although I cannot see him in the darkness, I envision his features to be twisted into a frown of confusion, brow creased with deep lines as he thinks of what to do next.
CALL THE POLICE. AN AMBULANCE. CALL A FUCKING FIRE TRUCK.
He doesn't speak, simply stands up and half-limps, half-creeps towards the doorway. I keep my eyes closed tightly, scrunched up as if what I cannot see cannot possibly hurt me. I'm too tired and in too much pain to speak, even though it fills me with dread to hear the horrendous noises of Beau murder yet another human with her bare hands.
"Hope," Abdul whispers into the darkness, his low voice barely reaching my eardrums. "I need you to shout as loudly as you can. You need to get their attention."
I remain silent, my conscious slowly fading in and out of blurry, quickly disintegrating reality. I imagine myself on a lilo, floating in a crystal blue swimming pool as the rays of the sun roast my skin. A few minutes must go by because the next thing I know, my eyes have opened, and Abdul's face is so close to mine that the tips of

our noses are touching. Stagnant, moist breath billows from his lips and attacks my nostrils, his bloodshot eyes staring deep into my soul. I shudder beneath him.

"I'm sorry to have to do this," he whispers solemnly.

My brow furrows just as he withdraws, and I see the outline of him reaching into a bag to get what appears to be a small, medicine-style vial. My eyelids grow heavier, and my eyes briefly close, shading my vision so that everything goes black again.

A bottle top being twisted. Liquid plummeted upside down.

The most excruciating pain I have ever experienced.

"FUCK!" I screech, my entire body jolting, on fire with agony. My body folds into itself like a deck chair, and I hold on to my throbbing leg. Light suddenly floods the room, and I look down in horror at the sizzling burn marks scorching through the material of my clothes. Raw, angry red flesh shines up at me, glinting smugly. The wound continues to fester and sting, its torturous heat burning my palms as I try to touch the skin.

I am too busy crying to hear Beau pounding down the corridor and only sense her leering over me in the doorway at the last moment. With eyes full of tears, I look up at her and wonder if there is any tiny shred of humanity somewhere buried beneath her thick, inhuman exterior. Is there any part of her that looks at me as her little baby sister? On death's door? I guess not when she throws back her head and releases an ear-shattering shriek, then bounds towards me like a rabies-riddled wild dog.

Sobbing, I squeeze my eyes shut and wait. But nothing prepares me for the horrendous BANG! That suddenly erupts into the atmosphere and explodes in every crevice of my skull. I look for just a split second, and I see Beau crash down to the floor for the second time that evening. Behind her, I see two figures wrestling, struggling down to the ground on top of her.

Either from pain or blood loss, I soon fall unconscious.

Faith

"Wake up."

In my sleep, I startle at the abruptness of the voice commanding me and flinch at the sharp dig to my side. My body hunches on the cold, damp ground beneath me, and I force open my eyes. Straight away, I close them again, the blinding light like a dagger to my pupils, the pain surging into the back of my head.

Shakily I jerk my head to the places where my skin burns. I wince involuntarily at the flash of the bright, angry red scalds festering on my flesh. I remember the shriek of pain and terror as the boiling water slapped over me and the look of twisted hatred on Mischa's face as she watched me suffer and writhe.

"I said, wake up," the voice repeats itself, and there is another kick, this time in the back of my shoulder blade. I yelp in pain and blink. I realise, with horror, that I cannot move my wrists or ankles. I'm bound and naked. Exposed. Vulnerable.

"What the…" I croak, my throat parched. I glance around and see that I am… my face collapses into a frown of confusion. This cannot be real. It cannot be true. This is a nightmare.

I struggle in my restraints, flexing my limbs before gazing wide-eyed up at the man towering over me, eyes so dark and crazed that piss trickles between my legs. I breathe. This isn't real. None of it is happening. I'm invincible. Untouchable.

"Pig," I clear my throat, "what is this?" I squirm, "take these off right now."

Pig kneels down slowly beside me, his joints clicking as he settles so that I can see his face, and his hot breath is congealing on my sweating cheeks. "Certainly," he smiles. "But first of all, we are going to play a little game. In actual fact, there are quite a few. Every time you win one game, you unlock a new piece of freedom. How does that sound?"

I seethe, rage bubbling uncontrollably beneath the surface.

"Fine," I mutter underneath my breath, teeth gritted tightly together. "What is it? And why the hell are we here?"

He licks his lip and glances around with a strange sort of fondness reflected in his iris. "Thought it might be nice to go back to where it all started. Happy memories, right, Faith?"

I blink around and have to bite my lip in case I say the wrong thing. I'm lying in the middle of the cold farm courtyard, the stench of stale animal shit still ingrained into the slabs of concrete combined with the stagnant odour of rotting animal carcass. I swallow a disgusting taste that stings the back of my throat and turn my head to look up at the tall, dark building that stands behind us. Its wooden planks are rotting, barely recognisable. It's painful, pitiful to look at.

Nothing compared to its former glory.

"What day is it?" I croak, my voice crackling. "Can I at least have some water?"

He pauses for a moment, then cocks his head and licks his lip. His eyes sparkle, just like they did that first night I met him. Before it got snuffed out.

"So glad you asked."

I watch as he turns around, and there is a heavy groan as he drags a metal tray around so that it is just a few inches from my face. My mouth becomes hot and sickly as it finally dawns on me what Pig wants me to do. Inside the tray, pale yellow water tinged with green congeals on the metal, severed pieces of rot floating like lily pads on the surface.

"I hope you're thirsty," Pig tells me quietly. Shoving the tray closer to me with his foot. "Because you're going to drink the whole thing if you want me to cut off the ties on your hands and feet. Seems fair, right?"

Biting my lip, I stare up at him with bitter eyes. "I never made anyone drink shit for no reason."

"Me neither," he snaps.

"I mean, I thought you understood the significance of my work," I tell him icily, "but evidently not. What is this, some kind of petty revenge ploy?"

He roughly grabs the back of my head by my hair. He yanks me upwards, then slams my face down hard into the trowel so that the steel edge cuts the bridge of my nose and chips unforgivingly at the bone. I scream, my mouth flooding with foul, stagnant liquid, quickly drowning in the vile substance, struggling for oxygen. Just when I'm about to pass out, he pulls me upwards again by my hair and drags me towards him so that I am forced to look into his cold, dark eyes, my sad, pathetic reflection staring back at me in their dark depths.

"Drink," he orders me, his voice firm, facial features sharp and hardened like razor blades.

I take a breath and do as he says. I'll play submissive. Make him think he's got all the control. Then, when he least expects it, I'll redeem myself, and he'll be fucking sorry. Sorry like all the others who dared ever to cross me.

It's harder than I anticipate, though. I used to have it tough, but that was a long, long time ago. I haven't needed to bide my time like this since I was just a defenceless kid. I lower my head to the disgusting surface of the water and am transported back to my weaker, less powerful former self. I breathe in the grotesque aroma of piss and decaying water. Bile scorches the back of my throat, but I force myself to open wide and let the mixture enter me.

At first, it's a sick kind of relief to drink. But soon, it starts to feel like poison, and I'm vomiting uncontrollably into the water, streaks of it splashing back upwards and plastering my cheeks.

"That's disgusting," Pig hisses down at me, kicking me hard in the stomach so that I keel over onto the ground, my shoulder blade splitting open against the dirty concrete. "I can't even watch you. Not nice though, is it Faith?"

I furiously blink back tears, determined not to show weakness. I make myself rigid, masking the pain and humiliation now stirring inside my chest.

Pig squats down, and I feel his dark, vengeful eyes scanning every inch of my naked, filthy body. My skin sizzles unpleasantly. He retrieves something from his pocket and playfully taps my sweating forehead with a small paper packet of something before ripping it open and holding it up so that I can see.

"You used to love throwing boiling liquids over people, didn't you, Faith?" he says before lowering the packet and sprinkling salt into the raw, skinless burn that gapes on my chest.

I scream. I can't help it. The pain is too much. Pig smiles, his lip curling upwards, eyes shining with delight. "Go on, beg me."

I shake my head, tears streaming down my cheeks. "Fuck off."

He laughs and tosses the empty salt packet to the side, standing up and grabbing me again by my hair so that I am forced to half-stand. "You're right," he tells me, panting slightly as he begins to drag me along, the rough ground skinning the soles of my feet as we stagger together away from the trough. "Begging never did any of us any favours, did it?"

I scan the morning-lit area all around me, the familiar farmyard eerie to me as we stalk through it towards the decrepit farmhouse. How can I escape? How can I get out of this? I take a deep breath and squint my eyes shut. *It's going to be fine. It's all going to be fine.*

Pig

The adrenaline fills me with inhuman strength as I effortlessly haul Faith across the farm towards that God-awful slaughterhouse. It is the place I used to live and work. The place I watched people die, and the place where I chopped them up and ground them into animal feed. In a way, the memories are somehow comforting in a sick, twisted sense. Kind of like the feeling of returning home, even if home was a household full of abuse and terror. At least it's the known. At least there are no surprises.

"See, I remember when I woke up just like you, naked, trapped, covered in shit," I tell Faith between breaths, "scared out of my mind. Forced to drink shit. That was pretty terrible. So bad, I kind of thought there was no way it could get any worse…." I chuckle, shaking my head at the naivety of it. "Boy, was *I* wrong? Now, you get to see it for yourself…."

The slaughterhouse smells worse than it used to, which is a pretty impressive feat. An aroma of decaying flesh, fragments of rotting bone, and bodily fluids hangs over the place like a vast cloak, shrouding it in an awful fog that will never clear. "Not been used for a while," I tell Faith, my voice cracking the horrific atmosphere, "not been cleaned either. You can't just feel the ghosts lingering in the walls. You can smell them too…."

Her face remains frozen, lips tightly shut, eyes red and bloodshot as they twitch in an effort to stay straight-faced. I smirk to myself and drag her through the darkness, purposely allowing her naked body to bash into various instruments of torture and farming machinery left abandoned in the shadows. When we soon get to the familiar transparent flaps, yellowing with grime and age, there is a small, sharp shriek coming from within. My grin of pleasure intensifies, and I feel the place between my legs harden against Faith's clammy, quivering thigh.

"Turns out you can hear them as well," I whisper into her ear, unable to conceal my glee as I feel her breath quicken against me.

I push her hard through the curtain and into the only well-lit area in the entire outbuilding. She becomes limp and heavy, obviously in protest, but I only tighten my grip as I force her towards the huge, bloodied lump of meat hanging from one of the old, rusted hooks. Beside it, another naked figure, also saturated in dried blood and the fluid from leaking wounds, is strapped to one of the dirty metal tables, where I used to slice flesh from bone whilst a guard jabbed me in the arse with the barrel of a gun.

"No…" Faith croaks as I hold her head up, forcing her to take in the gruesome scene in front of her. I feel her heart pounding furiously in her chest, her ribs rattling in my arms.

"Go on," I hiss, spit erupting from my lips into her ear. "Beg me now." I throw her forwards so that she face plants the blood-splattered concrete in front of the meat hook, then use a knife to sever the cords around her wrists and ankles. I drag her upwards again to find that fresh scarlet liquid is bubbling in the corner of her mouth and dribbling down her cheek from the impact of the fall. I press the knife into her shaking palm and hold it there, then gesture to Beau's dead torso dangling from the metal hook in front of us.

Just like a piñata.

Her head is half-attached, lolling sadly to the side, bulbous eyeballs bulging from deformed, swollen sockets. The sight of it makes me giggle with excitement.

"You fucking killed her?" Faith gasps, staggering backwards on her feet, reeling from the revelation. I hop, skip and jump over to the metal table where Hope's skinny, teenage body is stretched out over the tin surface. She is drenched in sweat, her pretty eyes glittering up at me in a silent plea. Her shoulder has been gnawed on, demolished into a thick, hot, bloody tangle of human tissue and flesh. A foul-smelling substance still leaks from the gaping wound.

I withdraw the gun, and in one swift movement, shove it deep into Hope's jaw so that she chokes and splutters, and bile spews from her cracked lips.

"You need to cut her up," I warn Faith darkly, "or I blow your other kid's brains out." To demonstrate, I probe Hope's throat further until the girl's eyes pop out of her skull and froth emerges from her stretched lips. The gun vibrates in my hand as she retches.

Faith's mouth falls open, and I watch in delight as she stares down at the sharp blade in her hand. For once, that smug glint in her eye has been wiped out. My head spins. Giddy with excitement.

"Five seconds!" I bark impatiently at her. "We haven't got all day, Faith...." I rip the gun out of Hope's mouth so that she sputters blood up into the air.

"MUMMY!" she shrieks, wriggling frantically on the table. "MUMMY, HELP ME!"

Faith's face contorts, her wrinkles showing, deepening in her despair. She gives me one final look of disdain before raising the knife and running fast towards the hunk of meat. My jaw drops as I watch for the blade to slice through Beau's sagging, demolished breasts, but before she can slice the flesh, she stops abruptly and falls down to her knees with a heavy thud.

"Not... not *her*..." she weeps into the floor, the knife clattering to the ground as she clasps the leaking torso and clutches it to her chest. Entrails slither out and slap onto the ground, mocking the grieving mother.

"You hear that, Hope?" I whisper, staring the teenager straight in the face. "Mother doesn't give a fuck about you. Only..." I'm cut off, and a blinding pain slashes fast through my side. Adrenaline bolts through me, masking the pain, and I turn in time to grab the sides of Faith's face and push her down to the ground.

I cackle maniacally as I grip her cheeks tightly and repeatedly smash her head against the concrete. I watch the veins beneath her skin expand and explode under her skin, and her eyes grow wild and desperate. I feel her skull shatter with each movement, the shards disintegrating between my hands. Even when I feel the life escape her pathetic shell of a body, I continue to smack it against the ground, laughing louder and louder, until suddenly I can no longer feel my arms.

Then, I fall backwards and let myself lay on the cold, bloody ground. With a heavy chest, I wheeze up at the ceiling and feel hot, salty tears welling up behind my eyes. My hysterical laughter dissolves into a hysterical fit of misery and rage.

I sit up, my cheeks wet with my feelings.

I pick up the gun.

I put it in my throat.

One year later

THE HORRIFYING TRUTH: A YEAR ON

Last summer, worldwide known animal rights activist and beloved pharmaceutical tycoon Faith Farmer was finally exposed for her brutal, sadistic reign of terror that lasted over a decade in the British countryside. An inquest into the suspicious circumstances surrounding the mogul's death revealed that instances of money laundering, identity fraud, and government corruption were just the tip of the iceberg for this outrageous woman. Aside from her financial and business misdemeanours, it transpires that Farmer was also guilty of hundreds of brutal kidnappings and murders. These crimes came as part of an underground business operation she led over two decades ago, involving using real human meat to produce animal food for a charity she ran under an alias. In addition, authorities have also found substantial evidence that Farmer would host live shows, where wealthy customers would pay to watch others being brutally tortured in an endless list of horrific, sadistic ways. The investigation is still ongoing, but according to lead detective DCI Regan Waters, progress is rapid, and authorities are locking down quickly on all of those involved in aiding Ms. Farmer's heinous crimes. These include the corrupted police forces involved in turning a blind eye to Farmer's operation, members of Farmer's cult reported 'cult following' and employees, as well as the individuals who paid for Farmer's services. There are currently six known survivors retrieved from Farmer's laboratory facility, in addition to a captive originally kidnapped by Farmer twenty years ago.

Mr. Abdul Chaudhary was drugged and made a prisoner by Ms. Farmer and has been held against his will ever since, subject to vicious torment and abuse. He gives a full, harrowing account of his experience in his book: '*Surviving the Farm,*' now available at all major book retailers.

Hope

It rains on the anniversary of their deaths.

In the dead midst of a summer heatwave, it seems apt that the sky would just suddenly open up, and a storm would break. It's as though mother herself has risen from hell or descended from heaven, causing more chaos yet, even in death.

Rainfall sloshes down over me, saturating my skin until I am shivering cross-legged on the enclosed lawn, my skin sticking to me, clinging onto my pale flesh. Underneath my palms, I feel the soil soften, and my hands begin to sink down into the earth. The scent of nature fills my lungs. The sky darkens rapidly. Through the blur of rain, I blink at the two humble, marble stones embedded into the grass, the engraved names so small and basic that I cannot read them.

Neither of them got a funeral. Unsurprising, considering I was the only thing that either of them truly had. Mother destroyed everyone else, ripping them easily from this earth, like buttons from a cotton shirt until I was the only thing left. And even then, I was barely clinging to life by the time she was finished with me. In the cold wind, the broken, jagged outlines of my scars split and weep. I've had multiple skin grafts, but it's never enough. Not enough to patch me up, to sew up the gaping hole that my sister gnawed out of me.

When the rain turns to hail and starts to sting the tops of my shoulders, I sigh heavily and stand. The soles of my bare feet sink into the mud as I hurry back up the lawn surrounded by its tall hedges and usher myself back through the sliding doors into my modest bungalow. It's a quaint place, but it's quiet and secluded, which is just what I need. A peaceful life, away from all the noise and chaos.

Without drying myself, I close the door behind me and sink into my single armchair, lifting a spliff to my lips and inhaling the familiar aroma. With my other hand, I pick up the fresh, hardback book that rests on my end table and lift it so that I can stare at the shiny cover once more. I take another deep drag of the joint until there is a low hum in the back of my brain.

Abdul's solemn expression stares back at me from the cover, his deep, intent brown eyes watching me carefully. Unmoving. A shiver runs down my spine, and the horrifying memory of his gun being shoved down my throat flashes through my head like the brutal replaying of a horror movie. Instantly, I drop the book.

I can't bring myself to open it.

We made a deal, Abdul and me. To support each other's claims.

I'd allow him to go public, go to the authorities and tell his story and expose my mother for all of her heinous, despicable acts. In exchange, I got a new identity, tucked away in a rural part of Wales, with my fair share of the inheritance. It's less than ideal seeing your mother's face splattered all over the news and multiple documentaries cropping up on Netflix about the horrifying truth that was her legacy.

Alas, I've long since realised that when your mother is the sick, sadistic mastermind behind over five hundred (and counting) individual murders, it's important to cut your losses.

Breathing out, I balance the joint in my ashtray and sit, listening to the rain streaming down the glass of the windows. Although I'm alone, cut off from the world, not even a real, functioning person anymore, I feel safe.

Who knows? Maybe one day, I'll go back out into the world. I've got enough money to be whatever I want.

I reach out for the half-full package of cold sausage meat, still laying discarded on the end table. I tilt back my head and let the seasoned meat slide into my mouth and down my throat.

Abdul

"She's pregnant."

I cough awkwardly and cock my head, feigning interest. In front of me, a grey-faced shadow of what used to be a human is slumped in a high-backed chair. Clumps of her hair are torn out, exposing red slivers of a scalp. Her body is so skinny; she looks like she might break if she tries to move. Her eyes are open but glassy and empty. Void of any kind of life. Void of any humanity. If Mischa is pleased about being with child, she certainly doesn't show it. If she's unhappy, she doesn't show it either.

Beside her, Mischa's mother, a stout woman with a big mouth and significantly smaller brain, tuts and shakes her head. In the background, I sense Mischa's father and various other family members lingering, pretending to watch TV, but keeping a very close eye on me.

"Congratulations," I tell Mischa, with a small, half-hearted smile that I know she will not even comprehend. I don't point out to the mother that it is most likely, with all things considered, that Mischa has been the victim of some sort of sexual violence. She does not even speak. She barely even breathes. Honestly, is it any wonder the girl was so quick to accept Faith? So attached to Jace? Just a poor, abused little girl trying to escape.

Trying to make this ugly world a better place.

"So, a million copies sold, I hear," Mischa's mother turns to me, clasping her fat hands together as she changes the subject. "Well done you. Amazing."

"Doing pretty well for yourself," I hear Mischa's father chime in behind me. "If only our Mischa could stop being so down in the dumps, she'd be able to get a book deal as well."

I try to meet Mischa's eye. There is no flicker, no vague trace of a reaction there.

She's gone.

I know that beneath her baggy, oversized clothes, horrific scars cover the majority of her body. I know that the scars on the inside are even worse. Severe post-traumatic stress disorder. That's what the doctors say. They pump her with drugs, but nothing seems to work.

Personally, I think she would be better off dead.

I quickly say my goodbyes to Mischa's insufferable family, get into the pretentious new car waiting for me on their driveway, and speed off away as fast as possible.

Life has been a crazy whirlwind since that day, one year ago, when I finally escaped Faith. I officially became a survivor. The *first* survivor of the farm, which has quickly become the most famous in the entire world. Even after they bulldozed the thing down, people still travel far and wide to go and visit and ogle at the place where hundreds were murdered and butchered into dog food. Needless to say, my book deal was snapped up immediately, and now I'm richer than I ever imagined I could be, even in the time before. They want to make a fucking film based on my memoir.

I'm famous.

If my parents were still alive, I'm sure they would be so proud. Dad died of cancer three months before I came home. Mum killed herself when she found out what happened to me.

Honestly, it stuns and amazes me how easily the world believed my story. I guess there was evidence aplenty, once the authorities knew exactly where to look. Once the story was taken out of that small, desolate little area of rural England that Faith had inhabited and infected with her evil.

Great for the local village's economy, I guess.

In spite of the fame and the money, I tend to keep myself to myself these days. I've frankly had enough of humanity for a million lifetimes. Honestly, the visits to brain-dead Mischa are more a case of keeping up appearances as opposed to actually caring. Why would I want to see the human, living embodiment of my trauma, staring darkly into space, reflecting back the horrors of my past?

No… I've had enough pain.

Now, my life (what is left of it) is all about maintaining pleasure.

The journey from Mischa's takes me about forty-five minutes. I turn down a long, wide cul-de-sac lined with lavishly decorated mansions mirroring one another. Unlike Faith's old place, it's a proper neighbourhood, so although I live alone, I'm not *all* alone, lost out there somewhere in the wilderness. There are other islands surrounding mine.

I drive slowly up the road and turn right towards the high, spear-topped iron gates surrounding the acres of land around my house. I let myself in using my key fob and yawn, tapping my fingers against the window ledge as I wait for the gates to creak open.

It's a quiet neighbourhood, mainly filled with old, well-to-do couples, and then some younger families where the kids go to schools where they need to wear hats as part of the poncy uniform.

A few doors down, there's a floppy, blonde-haired kid who reeks of boyish teenage arrogance. He reminds me so much of Daddy. It's a good thing. Sometimes I wake up in a cold, wet sweat, dreaming of the awful end Daddy came to eventually. I found out, much later, after leaving the lab for the last time, that once I had released all of the patients, they'd got to him before the authorities could. With the camera footage destroyed, no one can say for 100% certain what happened to him. However, the fact that he was found still partially chained and with a mouthful of blood and splintered teeth is pretty damning evidence. When I wake up from those dreams, I feel a pang of guilt that I left the kid there to be attacked by crazed test subjects, to end up choking on his own mutilated tongue. Then I just look at that little, floppy-haired, private school prick from down the road.

It takes a weight off my chest.

Swinging my keys, I exit my car and walk up the drive towards my house, breathing in the fresh, early evening air. I let myself in and pull the seven or so bolt and locks covering the door. I kick off my shoes, then walk across the polished floorboards, straight to the centre of the house where the entrance to my specially fitted cellar lies.

Hardly anyone in England has a cellar, but when you're rich, I've discovered, you can have whatever you like.

Can even have it sound-proofed.

I whistle a tune from the radio to myself, carefully unlocking the door to the basement. I step gingerly into the dark, the fresh scent of new plaster like a fragrant flower to my nostrils. My mind briefly wonders what to have for dinner. I briefly entertain the thought of pizza. I'm still very skinny. Could do with fattening up, I tell myself as I close the cellar door behind me and turn the key once more in the lock. I brush my hand across the wall and flick the switch so that the entire lower deck of my abode floods with bright light.

As expected, with the illumination comes the whimpering. A low, muffled symphony of pathetic weeps.

At first, a few weeks back, they started out as loud, high-pitched shrieks. Blood-curdling pleads for help, for mercy. They always do. But, after time, the human spirit breaks. It crumbles. I know that better than anyone.

"I wish you'd scream more," I yawn, bored. I make my way down the metallic, state-of-the-art staircase I had fitted. In the centre of the wide space is a long floor-to-ceiling pole. Attached to it are three girls. Two of them are red-faced, crying as they sit upright in a pool of their own piss and shit, naked arms slashed with angry red gashes. Beside them, their friend is slumped over, eyes open but glassy and lifeless. Her skin has taken on that pale, waxy sheen.

Dead.

I groan and put my hands on my hips, my brown furrowing into a deep frown.

"Oh, Jesus..." I mumble, shaking my head. "You weren't supposed to *die* yet!" I'm exasperated.

Taking a few steps forwards, I pause in front of the other two girls who flinch and refuse to look me in the eye. One corner of my mouth curls upwards into a smile.

"The fun is only just beginning."

Thank you.

Dear Reader,

Thank you so much for reading the Farm triology. I truly hope you enjoyed the experience as much as I enjoyed writing it. Please, please, please leave a rating and a review (even if you thought it was total crap, but even better if you thought it was amazing!) It really helps me as a self-published author, and is totally free.

I am on Goodreads, Twitter and Instagram (@sianroseauthor).

I love to hear what readers think so please feel free to drop me a message! ☺

Until next time!

Lots of love,

Sian Rosé

xxx

Printed in Great Britain
by Amazon